# FUR-BODING SHADOWS

*A Wonder Cats Mystery Book 8*

## HARPER LIN

# CONTENTS

## UGLY CHERUB

"No, I'm not surprised you agreed to do this," Tom said as he balanced on the empty counter to string a line of red hearts from the ceiling. "You are a hopeless romantic. I know it."

"Hey, I'm just doing my job to help out. Aunt Astrid can't climb up on the counter, and Bea gets so gushy and gooey over Valentine's Day." I shook my head. "Even though she's my cousin and best friend, it's enough to make me want to slap her." I handed him a glittery red heart to hang from a tack already in the ceiling.

"You're not fooling me, Cath Greenstone. You are as romantic as they come."

Tom Warner was my boyfriend. It was still a little weird to say, but I was starting to get very used to it.

But that didn't stop me from playing tough. Like right now.

"The Brew-Ha-Ha Café decorates for every holiday. I did the same thing at Christmastime. You remember the pretty star hanging in the corner up front? I hung that," I said proudly.

"That was my favorite decoration," Tom said as he hopped off the counter with a thud.

I giggled. Tom wasn't the kind of guy I ever thought I'd end up with. He was handsome with wavy black hair. His job on the Wonder Falls Police Department kept him in excellent physical condition. He had a great sense of humor. But most importantly, he accepted me.

I'd guess it would be fairly easy for any guy to accept me if I were any girl. But when you said to a fellow, "By the way, I come from a family of witches," well, they had the tendency to not be so accepting. Tom wasn't like that.

I reached into one of the three large boxes that Bea had decorated with hearts and arrows. We had pulled them from the storage room. I was purposely ignoring Tom as he inched his way closer to me.

"If we don't get moving, this decorating is never going to get done," I insisted as I pulled out the red-and-pink bud vases that were to go on all the tables.

"Come on, Cath. Just one kiss?"

"Not until the work is done," I said flatly, pretending not to notice him.

"I can't concentrate." He continued advancing.

"I wanted to tell you that I suspected you might have a touch of ADHD. I think a professional evaluation might be in order." I nodded sympathetically.

"Oh no. That won't do. Only one thing will be able to calm my frayed nerves."

"Frayed nerves?"

"You've got me under your spell."

"I can't cast spells all by myself," I retorted. That was true. Not until I had the years of experience and nerves of steel like my aunt Astrid would I be able to. I was never a very motivated student in school, so I didn't see that ability coming to me anytime soon.

Tom didn't say anything else as he slunk up alongside me, slipped his arm around my waist, and pulled me toward him. I offered my cheek. He kissed me. As much as I would have liked to sit in a dark corner and act like a teenager with Tom, I suffered from self-induced guilt. If I didn't get these decorations up, Bea and Aunt Astrid would have to finish, and I didn't want that.

"Where do you think we should put the cupid cookie jar Bea found at a garage sale?" I lifted the perfectly tacky décor from the box, pulled away the tissue paper it was wrapped in, and held it up for Tom to admire.

"Yikes. That is one ugly cherub." He wrinkled his nose.

"Isn't it?"

"Something this ugly should go front and center. How about we set it in front of the cash register?" He took it from my hands. "That way, everyone who comes in will see it."

"That's a great idea," I said. "Usually, it gets stuck on a shelf above eye level. Last year, I put it in the kitchen, and Kevin kept bringing it out. He said the eyes followed him and it made him nervous. Oh, that reminds me!" I snapped my fingers and went around the counter and into the kitchen.

When I came back, Tom had positioned the grotesque, diapered, flesh-colored blob in front of the register. Its blue eyes were slightly crossed, and the blond curls looked more like barnacles than hair.

"What is that?" he asked, looking down on my tray.

"Kevin made blondies." I put the tray down and grabbed one. Kevin Baker was our baker. It was his desserts, as well as our healthy salads, sandwiches, and snacks, that made the Brew-Ha-Ha a step above the other cafés in town. He was a genius in the kitchen and almost always made too much food. That was what I liked about him the best. There was always something to take home.

"Nice." Tom's eyes widened. "I think we've worked hard enough to take a quick break."

"I concur, Mr. Warner." I set his blondie on a saucer behind the counter and got one for myself.

"Wait one second." Tom hopped up and dashed into the kitchen. It sounded as if the place was being ransacked back there, with pots being shifted and cutlery being dropped, and I thought I heard the cabinet doors slamming shut a couple of times.

I took a seat on one of the stools at the counter and swiveled around. The café was starting to look very lovely. There were hearts hanging from the ceiling and little red lights twinkling around the window. It did look romantic. In the boxes, there were still some vases and fake red roses and a grapevine wreath with glittery hearts all over it.

I especially liked the draping garland that Tom had helped put up. Just as I was about to call to him, I looked at the café window and saw a face staring in at me.

As I squinted, I recognized who it was.

"Blake?" I mumbled. He waved without smiling.

I hopped off the stool and walked to the door. I snapped the lock and opened the door.

"What are you doing out there?" I asked without saying hello.

"I'm on my way to Jake and Bea's place. I saw you sitting in here and thought I'd stop by."

"Yeah." I didn't let him in. I didn't want him to stay. I wanted to be alone with Tom, and seeing Blake made me think of that kiss underneath the mistletoe during the holidays. That needed to be forgotten as soon as possible. "Tom and I are decorating the café."

"Oh, Tom's here with you?"

"He's doing something in the kitchen." I jerked my thumb in that direction.

"He's helping you decorate?"

"Valentine's Day is coming up. It's kind of corny, but the café looks so nice."

"It's strange that the shape of the heart as we know it was really the shape of two human hearts sewn together," Blake stated.

"That's charming."

"During the reign of Claudius II, marriage was outlawed so more men could be recruited to war. St. Valentine, under the cloak of darkness, continued to marry people. Of course, when they caught him, he was beaten and then beheaded. At least, that is one of the histories of why we celebrate Valentine's Day."

I stood there and looked at Blake. He nodded and looked past me at all the decorations. Finally, his eyes met mine. He looked cute in that nerdy way of his. I chuckled and rolled my eyes.

"You liked that one? I've got more."

"I'll bet you do. But Tom and I have to finish here," I replied.

With a curt nod and a quick good night, Blake was gone. That worked out fine because just as I was locking the door, Tom returned from the kitchen.

"It took a little more investigating than I thought it would, but I found it."

"What? Is this going to get me in trouble?" I asked while rubbing my hands together.

"You tell me."

Tom held up a can of whipped cream, a jar of red cherries, and chocolate syrup. My jaw fell open.

"Yes. That will get me in trouble. I'll really feel bad about it tomorrow. Really bad. I just hope I'll think it's worth it." I hopped back on my stool at the counter as Tom prepared our atomic blondies.

We sat together like kids at a soda fountain sharing a milkshake with two straws. It was romantic. It was fun. It was something I was completely unfamiliar with but was willing to learn.

"You've got a little whipped cream there." Tom pointed at my face with his fork.

"Where?"

"Here." He leaned over and kissed me gently on the cheek. I kissed him back on the lips. Yes, I was willing to learn.

## ❧ 2 ❧

## MARIE ELDERFLOWER

The next day, I got to the café early to start getting things rolling. The pots were full, and the entire place smelled like hot, strong coffee. Plastic cutlery were folded into napkins, ready to be dropped in with all of our take-out orders. The floor was swept of stray sparkles and shiny Valentine tinsel. I couldn't wait to see my aunt Astrid and cousin Bea's faces.

When they walked in, it was just the response I had hoped for.

"Cath, the whole place looks amazing!" Bea squealed. "I need to send a pic to Jake. Oh no! The cookie jar! That is perfect. It looks so romantically obnoxious."

"Put that thing back in the box," Aunt Astrid ordered.

"No way, Mom," Bea replied. "It is staying right here. To think I almost didn't go treasure hunting that day. I would have never found the cornerstone of our St. Valentine's Day décor."

The ladies fussed over everything Tom and I had done, from the garland of hearts across the ceiling to the red-and-white heart-shaped soaps in the bathroom to the folded red-and-white napkins.

I couldn't help it. I was proud of myself. Tom too, of course.

Bea brought some beautiful classical music to pipe through the speakers. When the customers came in, they felt the romance as much as we did.

The morning hustled by, as it usually did on a Friday. Before I knew what was happening, Bea and I were having a very heated debate over her food preferences and the dinner she'd be cooking at home that night. I hadn't decided if I was going to go or not. Based on her menu, I was leaning toward not.

"But what is it exactly?" I looked at my cousin. "Anything that can fake the taste of bacon isn't from this realm and probably shouldn't be digested."

"It's tofu, you big baby," Bea snapped. "It's very good for you."

In late January, Wonder Falls had two temperatures: cold, and windy and cold. This afternoon had morphed into the latter. Our busy morning slowed to a trickle of customers. That gave Bea and me time to focus on our differences and tease each other about them.

My beautiful cousin had an obsession with eating healthily. I'd never tell her to her face that most of her dishes were delicious. But I had a problem with tofu. There was no getting around it. It was a sickly white color. It had no flavor by itself. Then there was the insidious characteristic that it could take on the flavor of anything you wanted it to taste like.

"Yes, I understand that, but tell me again what tofu is."

"It's bean curd." She smirked as she stirred her new vegan chocolate frosting to slather all over our cupcakes before the lunchtime rush hit the café. "Plain, old-fashioned bean curd."

"So why don't they just call it bean curd?" I put my hand on my hip and watched her whip the frosting. "I'll tell you why. Because if they did, people wouldn't eat it. They have to put a fancy spin on it to get anyone to buy the stuff. 'Here, eat some tofu. Would you like a little more tofu? The president of the United States was seen enjoying some tofu.' You know what else they had to rename so people would eat it? Soylent Green. Why? Because it's people!

*People!*" I did my best Charlton Heston impersonation. It was pretty bad.

Bea tried not to laugh but was unsuccessful.

"So are you going to join us for supper tonight or not?"

"I think I'm going to take a pass. There are a couple cans of Chef Boyardee beefaroni in my cupboard that would hit the spot."

Bea shivered and wrinkled her face.

As I laughed, the door flew open with a frigid gust, a few puffs of blowing snow, and the mail lady.

Diane had been our mail lady for years. For as long as I could remember, she had reeked of cigarettes, walked partially hunched over with a weightlifter's belt around her waist, and growled her good mornings.

"Hi, Diane," I chirped. "What have you got for me today?"

"Mail," she grumbled and handed a bundle over to Bea, who was reaching for it. Diane's lips were thin and gray like the rest of her wrinkled skin. She leaned on the counter for a second to adjust her socks beneath her heavy boots.

"Diane, would you like a coffee for the road, on the house?" Bea offered. She tried to place her hand on Diane's. But the old woman would have none of it.

Unless the old woman had a sixth sense and knew Bea was an empath, which I'm pretty sure she didn't, that meant she just didn't like the lot of us.

"How am I going to deliver the mail with one hand?" Diane snapped.

Without skipping a beat, Bea leaned against the counter.

"If you put your cigarette down, you can hold your coffee," she said sweetly.

"Huh. That'll be the day." She snatched the mail from Bea and handed it to Aunt Astrid, who was sitting at her favorite table, counting receipts and balancing the books. "Your daughter is a little off, Astrid."

"We know," I piped up.

"The cousin isn't right either," Diane added without giving me a second look.

"We all have our burdens, Diane." Aunt Astrid was trying not to laugh. For all these years, Diane had been complaining about what bad kids Bea and I were. We had smart mouths and attitudes, and we dressed funny and giggled too much, and there was a long list of other offenses.

"Isn't that the truth? See you tomorrow." She turned and slouched her way toward the door.

"You're a ray of sunshine, Diane!" I yelled. "See you tomorrow!"

With a huff and a shrug, she walked out the door.

"And to think she's been married for over thirty-five years to the same man."

Aunt Astrid shook her head as she gave all the envelopes back to Bea and kept the *Wonder Falls Gazette* for herself.

"He's got to be the nicest guy in the world," Bea said.

"Well, that's always how it goes. Real shrews always get the nice guys. Look at you and Jake," I teased.

"Oh, hardy-har-har. Aren't you funny? What about you and Tom? He's as sweet as they come, and... look at you blushing. Mom, look at Cath. She's blushing like a virgin in the lingerie department."

"Bea!" I gasped and pinched her arm. "I am not blushing."

"No, you're just as red as those hearts hanging over your head."

"You don't know what you're talking about. Why

don't you just focus on your own love life and not worry about mine?"

"So, it's not just dating—it's a love life?"

"Aunt Astrid, Bea's teasing me, and she won't stop," I whined like a six-year-old. "Now she's looking at me. Bea, quit looking at me!"

"Mom! Cath is touching me!"

"Was not!"

"Was too!"

We laughed, but it only took a second to see Aunt Astrid wasn't.

"Oh no," my aunt said sadly.

My cousin and I both stopped our antics and asked what was the matter.

"Marie Elderflower passed away," Aunt Astrid said and held up the page of obituaries.

"Who is that?" I asked.

"She was a cousin of mine. Far, far down the line through marriage."

"Did we ever meet her?" Bea asked.

"I don't think so," Aunt Astrid replied thoughtfully. "She and I met at the library. We had started talking about a solar eclipse that was coming up. She mentioned hearing a rumor about a relative of hers who would carry on during certain lunar cycles."

"Like a lycanthrope?" I asked.

"Oh no. She was describing my great-great uncle Simon. He suffered from serious reactions to specific lunar cycles. Almost like an allergy. Most of us just thought he liked to run through the woods naked. But he claimed differently." My aunt shook her head. "Anyway, Marie had heard the story through her mother-in-law, who said it was a part of the family with questionable lineage."

"What does that mean?" I asked.

Looking around the café, Aunt Astrid scooted her chair closer to us and continued.

"In some instances, when the witches were trying to set up new lives for themselves, undetected, they went to safe houses and sometimes became part of another family."

"The Elderflowers are witches?" Bea asked.

"No. Not as far as I know. But they had this casual crossing of family lines with great-great-uncle Simon. I'm sure if I'd had more time to talk with Marie, I would have found out more. But she had kids too. In fact, she had two girls and then a surprise baby girl when the two other daughters were finishing grade school."

"How come we never met any of them?" Bea asked.

"Like I said, I only saw Marie the few times I

ran into her at the library. Then she had that miracle baby. The next thing you know, your time is all gone and so is your energy. Your kids steal it all."

"So if she had a baby late in life, how old was she?" Bea asked.

"According to this, she was fifty-four years old." Aunt Astrid's voice was sad. "Survived by her three daughters and husband. My goodness."

"So her youngest is a teenager?" I asked. I knew how it felt to have a mother taken away at a time when you really needed her. I had been nine when my mother was pulled underneath my bed by those horrible, scaly claws. The thought made my chest tighten.

"It sounds that way, honey," my aunt replied. "The wake is tomorrow morning. I think I'm going to go."

"We'll go with you, Mom. What time is the viewing?"

"Says here... am I reading this right? Does that say eight thirty in the morning?" Aunt Astrid handed the newspaper to Bea.

"That's what it says." She shrugged. "Maybe that was the best they could do on such short notice."

We all agreed that a wake at eight thirty in the

morning was a bit unusual, but the death of a woman in her mid-fifties was anything but the norm.

"What did she die of?" I asked. My gut told me cancer was probably the culprit. It seemed to have a way of getting people right in the middle of life.

"Hmm. This is odd," Bea said as she read. "It says here natural causes."

I looked at my aunt and waited for an explanation to that, but she looked as surprised as I was.

"Well, I didn't know her well enough to know her medical history," she offered humbly. "I would have liked to get to know her better. Each time we spoke, we found we had something else in common. Plus, she had a wonderful sense of humor. More than once, the librarians gave us a stern glare to quiet us down."

I felt bad for my aunt. I could tell she was sorry she didn't get to know this Marie Elderflower a little better. Especially knowing they were related somewhere down the line.

"Well, I think a visit to the wake would be a nice gesture." She continued studying the newspaper.

Bea and I agreed. We went back to work, but it was obvious we all had questions about this. If I knew Bea, and I thought I did, I knew she was wondering how she might have been able to help by using her gift of healing.

Aunt Astrid was probably planning to get to know the family a little better to at least offer some comfort through what would be a difficult transition.

I wasn't sure what to feel. I didn't know these people. My gift of communicating with animals didn't really seem to come in handy here. But maybe, if I could talk with the daughter, I might find the words that would bring her some kind of hope. I wasn't banking on it.

## 3
### FUNERAL

Collins Funeral Home looked more like a banquet hall than a funeral home. I wondered where the term *funeral home* came from. It was terribly morbid, which I guessed was appropriate.

"Is breakfast being served at this thing?" I asked while I tugged at the black skirt I was wearing. It was a simple A-line style, and I wore a white turtleneck on top.

Bea looked lovely in a black skirt that came down to her ankles, and she topped it off with a gray blouse. Aunt Astrid wore a navy-blue pair of wide-legged pants with a matching blouse that was flowing and loose-fitting. We had all cleaned up pretty well.

"I don't think so," Aunt Astrid answered. "But

there might be coffee and cookies or sweet rolls or something."

Bea had driven. Since there had been a dusting of snow, the town had sprinkled salt all over the roads. That was enough for Bea to stay a steady ten miles below the speed limit as she white-knuckled it the entire way there.

The parking lot was completely cleared of any snow as we crossed to the front door. The sky was a landscape of white, puffy clouds. Not gloomy but still perfect for a funeral. I trotted ahead and got the door. The wave of warm air from inside was as inviting as the smell of turkey on Thanksgiving.

"Boy, this place is as quiet as a tomb," I joked to Bea, who rolled her eyes as she walked past me.

Truthfully, it was. There were a few people in the lobby who looked us over as we walked in.

"Is it just me, or are we a little overdressed?"

The majority of folks here were in jeans or slacks. Several had red eyes and gave us a courteous nod as we made our way to the only viewing room with a casket in it.

"The Elderflowers weren't wealthy people," Aunt Astrid whispered. "They weren't poor, but you know how it is."

Bea and I both nodded. We had bills to pay. I

knew if the air conditioning at my house went out or my fridge gave up, I'd be eating ramen noodles and toast for several weeks before getting back on track.

I took off my coat and folded it over my arm as I let my aunt go ahead. She walked into the viewing room first. It was small. The casket took up the entire front of the room. There were four rows of eight folding chairs.

In the first row was a weary rag doll of a man sitting there, staring into space. I assumed he was Mr. Elderflower. He looked pale, and his eyes were sunken. Next to him, holding his hand, had to be the teenage daughter. She had dyed her hair black to match her nails and her lipstick. Her eyes were red from crying. All the layers of Goth makeup and clothes couldn't cover the fact she was still a child, and her mother was dead.

The only people speaking were two formally dressed women standing at the head of the casket. When I looked at the body of Mrs. Elderflower and then at the women, I knew they were her other daughters.

Both of them wore professional attire, as though they were heading off to traffic court or a job interview as soon as this whole ordeal was done. They looked at Bea and me suspiciously and then focused on Aunt Astrid.

"You must be Marie's daughters," Aunt Astrid said gently. She explained how she knew Marie and extended her hand to the ladies after introducing Bea and me.

"It's nice to meet you, Astrid. My name is Fern Elderflower. This is my sister Gail." Both women looked intently at us. They had not been crying. Their hair and makeup looked flawless. "We appreciate you coming. Mom had been sick for so long."

"May I ask what took her?" Aunt Astrid asked. I leaned a little closer to hear.

"It was just one of those things," Fern said. "She'd been declining for some time. There was nothing anyone could do about it."

I wasn't the only one who thought Fern didn't really answer the question. But we were strangers to the Elderflowers. There was no need for them to open up to us at all. Still, I watched their eyes as they spoke. They kept snapping past me to their Goth sister.

"Where is she going now?" Gail whispered to Fern.

I turned to see what they were looking at and saw

their sister get up abruptly and stomp out of the room.

"I'll go get her for you," I said without thinking. Before the Elderflower sisters could stop me, I was walking out of the room and toward the kitchen. When I got there, I saw the teenager standing at the coffee pot, just staring.

"Would you like a cup, honey?" I asked.

"I can pour my own coffee," she hissed.

"I-I know," I stuttered. "I didn't mean anything by it." I took a deep breath. I had been bitter toward people who tried to help when I lost my mom. What was it that made me feel better? What did I want someone to say that would have made me exhale for just a second? Nothing came to mind.

She carefully poured herself a small Styrofoam cup and then sat down at the small kitchen table. She still hadn't looked at my face.

"What is your name?" I asked.

"Evelyn. Who the hell are you?"

"Cath Greenstone. I didn't know your mom. My aunt did. She said she was a really nice lady and that there was a chance our families may have been related. Aren't we lucky?"

The teenager looked at me and curled her upper lip in disgust then shrugged.

"I lost my mom when I was nine," I blurted out. "I saw her go right in front of me. I can still see it." I didn't tell her I saw her get pulled away from me under my bed. "She was young too."

I waited and held my breath.

"Yeah, well, at least you weren't the cause of your mom dying," Evelyn spat, her eyes brimming with fresh tears. Her lip trembled, but she stopped it as she took a gulp of the steaming coffee.

"Evelyn, your sisters told us your mom had been sick for a while. That isn't your fault."

"My sisters aren't the most reliable sources for information. But look at them, and look at me. Who'd believe what I had to say?" She flicked her tongue while making the devil symbol with her fingers.

She had no idea that her dress and attitude didn't scare me. Had it been any other occasion, I would have enjoyed her attitude and called her on it just for fun. But I let her think she was getting to me. Today wasn't the day to tell her she was wrong.

"I'd believe you, Evelyn. I'd probably believe you first."

She looked at me, and again, her eyes filled with tears.

"What do you know about it?" Her lips trembled.

I leaned over to her, smiled, and whispered kindly, "I know more than you think. Come by the Brew-Ha-Ha Café if you ever want to talk."

I went to the coffee pot to pour myself a cup, when I was startled out of my skin.

"There you are!" Gail cawed. "How many times do we have to tell you not to leave Dad? He's sitting out there all by himself."

"I'm sorry, Gail. I was talking to Evelyn. She was just being polite," I interrupted.

It was as if she hadn't even seen me until I spoke. "Fine." She flipped her long red hair behind her. "I think it's time you go back and sit with Dad. Don't you agree, Evelyn?" Gail tilted her head to the side and blinked.

Evelyn glared at her sister. Without saying another word to me, she stomped out of the kitchen, her combat boots clomping on the linoleum.

"She's been a problem for a long time," Gail said.

"Teenagers can be a handful," I offered as if I knew what raising a teenager was like. I had no idea. But I remembered what it was like to *be* a teenager. It was miserable.

"I don't know how our mother tolerated her. I really don't. I think she was scared of her, to be honest."

"Scared of her?" I was shocked. "She's just a little girl, really."

"Little girl? She's seventeen and hasn't been decent since the day she was born." Gail flipped her hair behind her. "If you'll excuse me, I need to get back to my family."

"Of course," I mumbled. Walking back to the viewing room, I wondered what had just happened. It was a stressful time. People reacted differently to death, especially a sudden one.

When I finally rejoined my family, I wanted to complain that there weren't any cookies or treats of any kind. Instead, I just took a seat next to my aunt and waited.

"How long are we staying?" I whispered.

"Not too much longer," she answered.

I followed her eyes. They were focused on Evelyn.

"There is something going on with that girl."

"I can see it too," Bea replied. "Like she's hiding something."

"Yes. Things are not as they seem here," Aunt Astrid said. I squinted but couldn't see anything but a teenager going through that rebellious stage.

It was the two sisters, Fern and Gail, who were weird to me. They didn't look as if they had cried at all. But even as I studied them, I could see they were just different but not necessarily up to anything bad. Some people wrapped themselves up in their work or studies in order to cope with bad news. They could focus their minds on anything but the trauma, and that helped them through it.

There were only about five other people sitting in the viewing room with us. Some from the lobby came in to quickly shake hands with Gail and Fern, but no one went out of their way to talk to Mr. Elderflower or Evelyn. I felt a pang in my heart for them. I saw Evelyn's shoulders shake as she cried again and laid her head on her father's shoulder. He didn't move. At least, from where I was sitting, I didn't see him respond to her. Again, I chalked it up to shock.

"If I could just get close enough to take her hand or something," Bea whispered. "I might be able to help her."

"Are you talking about Evelyn?" I asked.

Bea nodded.

"Good luck with that one. Attitude up to her eyeballs. Typical teenager who won't say anything nice, if she says anything at all. She's not ready to get close to anyone."

"How do you know?" Bea asked.

"Because that's how I was. You won't get her to

offer you a handshake, let alone a hug or something. Can't you tell just by looking at her?"

I watched Bea's eyes as she studied the back of Evelyn's head.

"I guess you're right." Bea folded her arms in defeat.

"I've seen enough," Aunt Astrid said sadly. "Let me go and give our condolences to Mr. Elderflower one last time, and then we can scoot."

Bea and I nodded and began to put our coats on as my aunt went to the first row of chairs in front of the casket, where Mr. Elderflower was seated. I saw Aunt Astrid say a few things. I couldn't hear her, but I saw that same kind look in her eyes and the same smile that made so many people come to the café for her advice or a reading or just to say hello.

You could imagine my surprise when Mr. Elderflower began to yell.

"She saw them again! I should have been there with her! I should never have left her!"

"Mr. Elderflower, it wasn't your fault," my aunt said soothingly as she reached for his hand. Before she could touch him, Gail and Fern dashed in front of her.

"She saw them, and I didn't believe her." He began to sob as he stared into space. Evelyn sat there, staring at her father with gray tears running down her cheeks. She didn't try to touch him or console him. She just cried.

"Thank you for coming, Mrs. Greenstone, but we think it might be best if you leave. We need to calm our father down," Fern ordered.

"But I didn't—"

"Thank you, Mrs. Greenstone," Gail snapped and stepped between Aunt Astrid and Mr. Elderflower as bodyguards might do to obnoxious paparazzi.

Bea hurried to her mother's side and linked her arm with her mother's. With quick apologies, she shuffled Aunt Astrid away from the excitement. I carried her coat and purse. Before we knew it, we were out in the parking lot, making our way to Bea's car. Half a dozen faces were pushed up against the glass of the funeral home, watching us leave.

"What was that all about?" I asked.

"I-I just went to shake his hand," Aunt Astrid stuttered. "I certainly didn't mean any disrespect."

"It isn't you, Mom."

"No, Aunt Astrid. Those people are probably still shaken up. They probably don't have any idea what they're doing or how they're behaving. Grief comes in all shapes and sizes."

"Do you really think that's all it is?" Aunt Astrid

took my hand to steady herself. "You didn't get the feeling there was something more going on?"

"I didn't," I admitted.

"I'm not sure what I think," Bea added. "But those people aren't normal."

"And we are?" I held the door open for my aunt to climb in the front seat. "I just think this is too delicate of a situation to make any judgments on the Elderflowers. Tomorrow, they could act completely different. I know when it was my mom..." A lump formed in my throat, but I choked it down.

"When I had to bury my mom, I didn't know what I wanted to do. I wanted to scream and swear and cry, and still, I wanted to be brave and careful. That's hard for a nine-year-old to process. I don't think another eight years would make it any easier."

There was the sting of tears in my eyes, but I managed to blink them back.

"I wasn't even thinking, Cath," Aunt Astrid said as she buckled herself in. "You should have waited at the café. This had to be painful for you. I'm so sorry."

"I'm all right, Aunt Astrid. Sure, it made me think of my mom. But that's why I think we should let the Elderflowers have some breathing room. Mr. Elderflower is feeling guilt, but it could be for not picking up milk at the grocery store that day. We don't know."

"You're right," Bea said. "But what do you think he meant when he said, 'She saw them again'?"

"I was wondering about that too," Aunt Astrid said.

"Who knows?" I answered. "Maybe he meant mice in the cellar or shapes in the clouds. I'll bet if you ask him again in a couple days, he won't even remember he said it."

"I'm thinking of doing just that. Perhaps a nice casserole would be a kind gesture," Aunt Astrid mused. She elbowed Bea, who I knew would be happy to cook something weird and delicious.

"Okay. But I bet you won't find out too much." I rubbed my aunt's shoulders affectionately from the back seat.

I'd been wrong before. But this was one of those times I was wrong on an epic scale.

## 4

# DOMESTIC DISTURBANCES

As I was locking up the café after a slow day, I heard a catcall from behind me.

"What do you think you are doing, Tom?" I said once I realized it was him.

"I'm coming to walk my best girl home before I head off to work. What do you think I'm doing?"

"Starting trouble," I replied with a smile as he leaned in for a kiss.

"Busy day?" he asked.

"No. This cold snap brings out only the bravest of souls. I think I sold two brownies and maybe six coffees all day. That's why Bea and Aunt Astrid went home early and I'm locking up." I turned the key in the door until I heard the thick snap of the dead bolt slipping into place. "Besides, they are on a mission."

"Oh yeah? What are they up to?"

I told Tom about the Elderflowers and the wake. He seemed more surprised than I expected.

"Why are you looking like that? They're just bringing over a casserole. People do that all the time."

"No. It's not that," Tom said. "I have been at the Elderflowers' home before. We've gotten calls from neighbors for domestic disturbances."

"What?" I clutched my imaginary pearls.

"Yeah. Over the past year, I've been there about four times. I recognize the name. Like Greenstone, it's pretty unique. Not a name you quickly forget."

I was shocked. "Mr. Elderflower seemed so frail and small at the funeral home. He was beside himself. I can't imagine him lashing out at his wife. In fact, he was blaming himself for her death." I filled Tom in on what had happened right before we left the wake.

"Well, that makes sense because he wasn't the aggressor." Tom raised his eyebrows.

"You mean Marie Elderflower was beating on her husband?"

"Maybe not beating but threatening. Pushing him around, maybe." Tom's voice was firm.

"That bothers you?" I slipped my arm through his as we slowly walked toward my house.

"Like I said, I was at the house a couple times." Tom shrugged. "I'd talk with Mr. Elderflower and tell him that leaving was an option. No one would begrudge him leaving with his youngest daughter to get away from a volatile situation."

"What did he say?"

"That he loved her. He couldn't leave her like this. It wasn't her fault."

"Was his daughter Evelyn there when these things happened?"

"Yes. It's no wonder that girl has turned out the way she has."

"Have you ever had any dealings with her being on the wrong side of the law?"

"No. But give it time. According to her sisters, Evelyn Elderflower will be on a path to destruction soon enough. Following in her mother's footsteps, I guess."

I looked down at the sidewalk and watched our feet as we strolled.

"You know, just because she wears black lipstick and acts all broody doesn't mean anything is wrong with Evelyn. She's just a kid." I looked to Tom for support.

"Maybe," he replied. "But with a violent home life and now that the stronger parent is dead, leaving the weaker one in place, well, she'll probably take over the role as abuser."

"Ugh! How can you be so negative?"

"I've seen it before, Cath." He shrugged. "It's sad, but it's one of those things that gets passed down to children. But who knows. There are always exceptions to the rules. I've also seen my fair share of miracles. I wouldn't rule anything out just yet. This ball game is too close to call."

He squeezed my arm, and we walked a little farther in silence. My mind was spinning. I couldn't imagine family beating on each other. The idea of it made my stomach flip over on itself.

I knew my aunt and cousin were bringing a casserole over to the Elderflowers' that night. I was thinking it might be a good idea for me to do the same. I'd pick up a coffee cake or something in the morning and slip by there. But I wouldn't tell anyone. Hopefully, Evelyn would answer the door, and I could have a few more minutes to talk to her.

"Well, here we are." Tom snapped me out of my trance at my front door.

"I meant to tell you that Aunt Astrid and Bea thought the café looked beautiful." I rocked back and forth on my heels.

"Well, I'm glad my interior-decorating skills

weren't a complete bust. The guys at the precinct find it a little weird. But then again, they've seen my girl and can't blame me for jumping through a few hoops in order to get you alone."

"Stop," I gushed. "You're embarrassing me."

"Embarrassing you? The prettiest girl in Wonder Falls?"

I couldn't help it. All the thoughts of the Elderflowers and their sad situation flew right out of my head as Tom kissed me on the front porch. Before I could forget my own name or how to unlock my front door, I felt a familiar push against my foot.

"Meow."

"Treacle. You silly kitty. What are you doing out on this cold night?" Tom said, scooping my big black cat up in his arms. Without hesitation, Treacle gave him an affectionate headbutt under the chin, his purring motor running full speed.

"He's got an open window when he wants to come back home. Don't you, big guy?" I scratched behind his ears before pulling out my keys to get inside. I hadn't been terribly cold until Tom mentioned it. Then I realized it was freezing outside.

He passed the big furry ball to me after I opened the door.

"Well, what do you say we have dinner tomorrow. A couple of burgers or maybe a pizza?"

"I think that sounds good." I smiled and stepped inside. The warmth of my house sent a shiver across my shoulders.

After one more kiss that lasted a couple minutes, I finally shut the door to the cold elements outside, turned up the heat, and shut Treacle's window for the night.

"*I like Tom,*" Treacle said telepathically as he hopped up on my bed and began his nightly grooming routine.

"I do too."

"*Do you think you'll marry him?*"

"What? Why would you ask that question?"

"*Curiosity and the cat. Blah, blah, blah. You know how the saying goes.*"

"I'm not thinking of marriage right now. What I'm thinking is that I need to find out a little more about this Elderflower family, and I'm not sure how to go about it."

"*Maybe I can help.*"

I thought for a minute and looked at Treacle. He yawned and sat up straight and proper, still purring happily.

"Maybe you can."

## 5

## A LITTLE BLOOD LEFT

"Well, I just don't know what to think," Bea said just as Treacle and I walked into the café.

"Don't know what to think about what?" I asked as I pulled off my coat, scarf, and hat. Treacle scooted over to the table by the heater, hopped up, and began to doze.

"We went to the Elderflowers' house last night. I made a lovely chicken potpie with biscuits, and Mom brought chocolate chip cookies for dessert," Bea answered.

"I love your chicken potpies," I said, pouting. "Don't tell me they didn't like it."

"We don't know," Aunt Astrid said. "Mr. Elderflower invited us in. He kept apologizing for the state of the house."

"What was wrong with it?"

"Nothing we could see at first," Bea said. "But as we helped him get set up, we saw that some pictures were facing backward on the walls. There were a lot of shadows, like a couple of bulbs had burned out and had yet to be replaced. But we couldn't find any bulbs that were out."

I looked at my aunt, who was pinching her lips together. "What about you? Did you see anything?"

"Nothing. For the first time in many years, all I saw was the room in front of me. There were no portals, no jutting angles, no clouded dimensions peeking through to this one. I saw his house with perfect vision."

"That *is* weird."

My aunt could not only see other dimensions but, with a touch of hocus-pocus, could actually submerge herself in some of them. That was why she walked so slowly. People had it in their heads she was old and slowing down. The truth was she was in fine health. It was her altered vision that made her step carefully. So, when she said she entered a place where the other dimensions were blocked from her view, that was not normal.

"Why do you think that is? Could there be a natural explanation for it?"

"Well, unless a small Cape-Cod-style house in the lower- to middle-class part of town is the nexus of the universe, I can't think of any reason why that would be." Aunt Astrid scratched her head.

The café was warming up nicely. Kevin was pulling a fresh batch of orange-cranberry muffins out of the oven. They smelled so good even I was ready to gobble them down. Usually, I adhered to a strict diet. If it had chocolate or vanilla frosting, I'd eat it. If it had fruit or veggies in it, you could bet I'd have to think about it.

"So, there is something a little strange about the Elderflowers' house." I tapped my chin. "Maybe it's built on an ancient Indian burial ground, or there is some electromagnetic pole centered there. Maybe an asteroid hit on that spot a million years ago and it affects the dimensions around it. I'm just thinking out loud."

"We did that too," Bea said. "After we were practically thrown out of the house on our... ears."

"What?" I gasped.

My aunt nodded and clicked her tongue. "But Mr. Elderflower invited you in. Then he threw you out?"

"Not him. His daughter," Bea replied.

"Which one?" I had assumed that it was Gail or Fern. They seemed very cold and very private at the viewing. I was shocked when Bea said it was Evelyn.

"She came in the house, slammed the door, and demanded to know what we were doing there," Bea continued. "Of course, I tried to talk her down off the ledge, but she was having none of that."

"What did she say?"

Aunt Astrid took a deep breath and explained. Evelyn had said they didn't need any do-gooders pushing their way into family business so they could gossip all around town.

"Mr. Elderflower sat down at the kitchen table with his head in his hands and said nothing," Bea added. "I wanted to go to him, but Evelyn started stomping around the house and telling us to get out, or she was going to call the police. There was no way I was going to put my hands on her father. I didn't want him to get hurt."

"Did you really think Evelyn would hurt him?" This pill wasn't going down.

"Let's just say I wasn't going to bet the odds that she wasn't." Bea shook her head sadly.

I looked over at Treacle, who had been listening to the whole story. I was having a hard time believing it. Of course, I knew my family wasn't lying. But there had to be more to what they were telling me. Something they didn't see.

"Thankfully, as we were scooting down the walkway, Gail showed up."

"What did she say?" I asked.

"She said she was there to check up on them. When we told her what happened, she nodded as if it were a normal occurrence and told us thanks for stopping by," Bea answered. "I wouldn't say either one of the Elderflowers' other daughters is an example of fine manners. They seem a bit rude. But if I had a mother who was suffering from violent dementia, a father who couldn't cope, and a younger sister gone wild, well, I might be rude too. To say the least."

"You think Evelyn has gone wild?"

"Well, Fern is a dermatologist with her own office, and Gail is a veterinarian with her own office," Aunt Astrid said. "They seem to be quite successful. If you saw the Cadillac SUV Gail pulled up in, you'd see she was doing pretty well too."

I was about to open my mouth and defend Evelyn to Bea and Aunt Astrid when Jake and Blake tapped on the glass door of the café.

"We're closed!" I yelled, standing in front of the

door. "We don't open for another minute! You'll have to wait!"

I put my hands on my hips then looked at my watch.

"Cath, I'm not above arresting family," Jake replied.

"Fine." I snapped the lock and turned over the Closed sign so it read Open. "I guess the rules don't apply to you. I didn't realize this was Jake's world and we were just in it." I huffed as I walked over to Treacle.

"This is a nice surprise." Aunt Astrid fussed over Blake as if he were her long-lost son. "Sit down, boys. Cath, get them some coffees to go. Blake, are you hungry?"

"I had some toast and coffee before I left the house this morning, Aunt Astrid. Thanks." He barely smiled, but his eyes twinkled.

"Nonsense. When it's cold outside, you have to give your stomach something to do. It will help keep you warm. Cath, go get a couple of Kevin's muffins for Blake."

"He just said he had breakfast." I stood there with my hands out, shrugging.

"He lied." Aunt Astrid gave him a wink. "Get him two of them, and put them in a to-go bag."

I let my arms fall and stomped to the kitchen.

"Hi, Kevin," I mumbled.

"Hey, Cath," he said with his cheeks rosy red from the heat of the ovens and the stove. "Would you mind cracking the back door for me?"

"Not at all."

Kevin often kept the door cracked to cool the kitchen off while he baked. The winter air would feel especially good this morning. As if on cue, Treacle hopped down from his table, stretched his legs, and trotted out the door.

*"I'll be back as soon as I can,"* he said as he slithered through the small space.

*"Be careful, and don't take any unnecessary risks."*

With Blake's orange-cranberry muffins in my hand, I returned to the front of the café.

"So, what are you guys up to today? Anything interesting?" I asked while I bagged the muffins, adding two pats of butter, a container of honey, red napkins with hearts on them, and a fork. Sure, I didn't have to put all those nice things in there, but the guy did only have toast for breakfast.

"We are actually heading over to Collins Funeral Home," Jake replied.

"That sounds like the beginning of a joke. Two

cops are on their way to a funeral home to inspect a body." I chuckled.

"I wish it were. But we got a strange call from the undertaker."

I handed Blake his breakfast and leaned closer.

"What kind of strange call?" Bea read my mind.

"Well, um, Blake? What would you say this is?" Jake turned to his partner and shrugged.

"It appears that the body of one of their patrons was defiled sometime in the night. We aren't sure what that means yet. Those are Mr. Collins's words. But he was very earnest that we come by and investigate."

"Did he say who the person was?" Bea asked, looking at her mother and then me.

"It was Marie Elderflower," Jake said. "But I don't need to tell you guys to keep it under wraps. Not for our sake but for Mr. Collins. Any rumor of a dead body being violated in any way at a funeral home will get the place shut down. We need to see exactly what he's talking about first."

I rubbed my stomach.

"No problem, Jake. Who would we tell anyway?" I held up my index finger. "Bea, pour me some of that tea, there. Add that lavender sprig."

She did it quickly and handed me a large to-go cup.

"Here. I'm not sure why, but this tea tastes good with these muffins." I looked up at Blake and, for the first time in a long time, didn't feel the urge to blush and run away to scribble about him in my diary.

Of course, all I got in return was a grunt and a nod.

"Please, be careful." Bea leaned over the counter to give Jake a quick peck on the cheek. "And let us know what you find out."

"Yeah. Let us know," I repeated. "Don't leave out any details."

"You're a weird one, Cath," Jake replied after kissing his wife.

"Takes one to know one."

"Now, you eat that before it gets cold, Blake. Be careful, you boys." Aunt Astrid waved as the guys left the store.

"Well, that is a strange turn of events." Bea put her hand on her hip. "I'm not sure what to think about that. I wonder where Evelyn Elderflower was last night. We know she came home for a spell, but that doesn't mean she stayed there."

"Mr. Collins has at least three people working at

his business. I hate to say it, but it could be any weirdo there."

"Cath is right. We can't just assume Evelyn is up to no good," Aunt Astrid said.

"Besides, just because she looks evil doesn't mean she is. We can't forget that she's only seventeen." I wasn't sure why I felt the need to defend this girl I didn't know. I guessed it was because I felt as though I did know her.

It was obvious Aunt Astrid and Bea were trying to look at things from all angles. But they had no idea what Evelyn was feeling. I didn't either, really, but I had a better idea because I had been there. All the witchcraft and spells and fortune-telling and crystal-gazing couldn't change the fact that Evelyn was broken. Not permanently. Not forever. But for now, she was functioning the way a seventeen-year-old girl should. It wasn't her fault. I just couldn't understand why no one saw this but me.

Once again, business was slow due to the cold weather. But one person was willing to brave the elements, wrapped in her full-length fur coat and leather boots with matching gloves.

"Hello, Darla. What brings you out on this chilly winter day?" Bea asked politely.

Darla Castellan was the Lex Luthor to my Superman. We had spent four hellacious years together in high school when I was the post she used to sharpen her claws on.

"Is it really that cold? I barely noticed." She tugged up the massive collar around her ears. "Just a small coffee with an orange-and-cranberry muffin. I'm actually meeting with my ex-husband."

"So there's still a little blood left in that corpse?" I knew it was mean and petty, but so was Darla, so I didn't see any harm.

"Shows how much you know. Darren Castellan has been trying to win me back ever since he signed the divorce papers." She flipped her long black hair behind her. "This is just another one of his emergency lunches at Arons in which he tells me that he still loves me and wants to give us another try."

She just had to drop the name Arons. It was just the chicest restaurant in town. Everyone who wanted to be seen was seen there. To sit at the bar and order a Coke would cost about twenty-five dollars and require reservations two months in advance. Naturally, I'd never been there.

"Well, good luck with that," Bea said cheerfully, handing Darla her change.

"I don't need luck. I always have the upper

hand." Without a thank-you, she turned and stomped out the door.

"Calm down." Bea smiled at me. "You know she just does that to aggravate you. I bet she's not even going to Arons. She just got all dressed up to make it look like she was going somewhere. She's probably heading back to her house to sit and eat her muffin along with a tub of rocky road ice cream."

I had to laugh. "I just can't let it go completely. Just when I thought I could totally forgive Darla for the torture she put me through, she shows up. It's very hard to not walk up and slap her."

"She's got your number, Cath," Aunt Astrid said as she took her seat at her table for two next to the counter. "Don't you think it's about time you change that number?"

"Maybe. But she's one of the few people I love to hate. The rest I just hate."

"You don't hate anyone," Bea said soothingly. "You are one of the most lovey-dovey people I know. Underneath that hard exterior is a gooey, chocolaty, sweet center of love."

"You're on crack." I grabbed a handful of forks and napkins and began to place them on all the tables.

"I saw you give Blake some honey and extra

butter. *Oh, try this tea. It goes so well with the muffin.*"
Bea teased in a singsongy voice while shaking her
hips and batting her eyelashes.

"Blake is like that obnoxious cousin you only see
at family get-togethers and is cross-eyed, but you try
to be nice and pretend you don't notice."

Aunt Astrid laughed out loud.

"Besides, Tom and I have been seeing quite a lot
of each other. I don't have time to worry about Blake.
He's got you and Jake and, my gosh, Aunt Astrid,
could you fawn all over him a little bit more?"

"What are you talking about?" She shrugged.

"You are always making a fuss over him." I
smirked. "You don't try to hide it. It's quite a
spectacle."

"He's a bachelor. He's got no family. And he's a
cop." Aunt Astrid counted off on her fingers. "That's
dangerous for a man already. A man who thinks he
doesn't have anyone worrying about him is lost. He's
got to know there are people who want him to come
home safe every night."

I couldn't argue with that. As much as he
annoyed me, I wanted him to come home safe every
night.

## ❧ 6 ❧

## LOST IN THE SHADOWS

The rest of the day, I kept an eye out for Treacle. He and I had devised a grand plan to do a little snooping around the Elderflower homestead. I told him to just get in and get out, but my cat never followed directions to the letter.

When he still hadn't arrived at closing time, I was beginning to worry. I panicked when I didn't find him at home either.

*"Treacle, didn't I say no unnecessary risks?"* I tried to communicate to him.

I grabbed the flashlight I kept by the front door, snapped it on, and went to the door that led to my laundry room. My house didn't have a full basement. Instead, it had a second level below ground big enough for the washer and dryer, a small freezer, and boxes of holiday decorations. The floor was concrete. The walls were dreary. I kept meaning to brighten it up a little with some paint or wall hangings or something but hadn't gotten around to it. The worst part of my secret room was that the light switch was all the way on the other side of room.

"Treacle?" I could see my breath in wispy steam. The window I left open for the cat was too small for a person to get through, but it was just right for the cat.

I saw something move out of the corner of my eye. When I swung the beam of light around, there was nothing there. As I focused on the corner, something else moved on the other side. The flashlight beam cut through the darkness, but still I saw nothing. Taking a deep breath, I stomped angrily over to the light switch and flipped on the overhead light. The room looked exactly the way I'd left it a couple days earlier after doing my laundry.

"Something is off." But I couldn't place it. I shined the flashlight behind the washer and dryer and freezer and boxes of decorations but found nothing but old spider webs, dust bunnies, and the occasional stinkbug carcass. When I shined the beam up to the window, two green eyes flashed at me.

"Meow!"

"Treacle! Get in here! I've been worried sick."

"*I need your help.*" He panted. He wouldn't slink through the window to jump in and onto the floor.

"What is it, honey?"

"*I can't make it.*" He collapsed.

"Treacle!" I shouted. Before I knew what I was doing, I had dashed up the stairs and out the front door to the tiny window at the back of the house. There was my cat, lying in the cold, brown grass. I scooped him up in my arms and quickly folded him into my shirt. "What happened to you?"

Once inside my house, I kicked the front door shut with the back of my shoe and brought Treacle into the kitchen.

"Are you all right? You're frozen to the bone!" I set him down on the table and grabbed a tea towel to rub his cold, wet paws. "What in the world happened? I was expecting you at the café. If I didn't think to go check in the laundry room, you might have frozen to death out there. Oh, my poor kitty."

It didn't take long for Treacle's purring to start. He shook his head a couple times and sat up.

"*I kept getting lost in the shadows,*" he finally said, giving my hand a tired nudge with his head. "*I went to the Elderflowers' house. As it turned out, there is a familiar living next door.*"

"Well, that was lucky." I scratched him behind the ears before pushing myself up from the table to get a small saucer for some milk.

*"Yes. His name was Hines. He had a cat door. I've always thought those were a little too fancy for me. But some felines like them. Hines was a Siamese. They are always a little high maintenance. Anyway, he said the woman next door…"*

"Mrs. Elderflower?"

*"Yes, Hines said she would come out of the house at night, yelling and cursing. Then she'd run from the back porch to stand under the light on the detached garage. She'd just stand there under the light at night, cursing."*

"That poor woman. It sounds like dementia."

*"That does. But the weird shadow forms don't."*

"What are you talking about?"

Treacle went on to tell me that Hines saw strange shadows on the Elderflower property.

*"He said that sometimes at night he'd see them move out of the corner of his eye but that only once did he see the eyes."*

"Eyes?"

*"He thought it was a rat. Rat eyes glint red sometimes. But these were too big. By the time Hines could get a good look, whatever it was disappeared."*

"That's weird."

*"Hines also said that, during the day, the house seemed*

like it was under a perpetual cloud. Like the sun just couldn't reach it."

"Did he say anything about the family other than Mrs. Elderflower?"

"The only thing he said about the family was that Mrs. Elderflower wasn't the only one who would have episodes in the yard. The daughter did too."

"Which daughter?"

"He didn't say."

"So. You want to tell me what happened to you?"

"I'm not really sure. All I know is that I kept getting lost in the shadows."

"On the way home?"

"Yes. When I left, Hines went back into his house. I saw something move near the neighboring house."

"The Elderflowers' house?"

"Yes. I thought it was a mouse. When I went to inspect it, I couldn't find anything at first. But you know how it is, Cath. You just take a few more steps. You don't always think about the steps you'll have to take back."

"Didn't I say, 'Don't take any unnecessary risks'?" I scratched him behind his ears and stroked his back.

"Would it help if I told you I wanted to bring the mouse home for you?"

"No. So what did you see?"

"Nothing. You know how your eyes need a second to

*adjust when the sun is glaring down in the summertime and all of a sudden you step into a dark place? It was like that. Except my eyes never could adjust."*

"For a cat's eyes never to adjust, that had to be some serious shadow."

*"It was. It was like a living thing. I had to try to retrace my steps out of there. But the shadow never lightened. That's why it took so long to get home. I was feeling my way through smoke."*

"How long were you outside the window?"

*"A long time."*

"Why didn't you just jump in?" I placed a saucer of milk in front of him.

*"Because I was afraid if I jumped into the shadow of the laundry room, it would swallow me up."*

I wrapped my arms around him and squeezed.

"You're home now. Home and safe." I gently gave him a headbutt. "Next time I say don't take any unnecessary risks, listen to me, okay?"

*"I learned my lesson."*

I cranked the heat up, tossed a couple of extra blankets on the bed, and let Treacle snuggle into them while I took a hot shower. While the water warmed me up, I thought about what Treacle had said.

Wonder Falls had some interesting patches of

weird property. There was the Suicide Bridge and the road that led to it that I hoped to never see again. There was the old Wonder Falls Orphanage that had sent a shiver up my spine. That my family and I were the only ones to know about the strange goings-on didn't change the fact that some old bits of land in Wonder Falls had loose soil on top. Some recent activity might have drummed up a resting spirit.

My heart sank a little as I stepped out of the shower and wrapped myself in a towel. It wasn't looking good for Evelyn. So often, teenagers turned to magic in an attempt to get ahold of their lives. And ninety-nine percent of the time, they had no idea what they were doing. They didn't consult anyone who might. Then they ended up unleashing a nightmare.

It was still too early to tell if she'd unleashed a nightmare. I scolded myself for being so dramatic. Still, with the death of her mother and a father who was too scared of her to stop her, I was convinced that Evelyn needed my help.

After I got into my warm flannel pajamas and went to my bedroom, I found Treacle sleeping peacefully. I turned on the television, and the original black-and-white version of *Cyrano de Bergerac* was on. Even though I thought I was too tired to read the subtitles, I managed to stay up to watch the big-nosed hero spill his heart out to Roxanne. They were in love with each other, flaws and all, for only the last few minutes of his life.

Okay, so I did cry when he drew his sword to fight his old enemies of cowardice and jealousy and despair. It made me think of Darla when she came to the café in her fur coat and perfect makeup.

"Don't let yourself fight cowardice and despair in the last few minutes of your life, Cath." I turned off the television and snuggled around Treacle, who had become an adorable black, fuzzy ball that weighed as much as a wet sandbag smack dab in the middle of the bed. When I touched him, his motor instantly kicked on.

"You've been through enough," I whispered. "I'll sleep around you."

It didn't take long for Treacle to get too hot in the blankets with my body generating even more heat next to him. I felt him stand, stretch, and yawn before venturing to the pillow and curling up around my head.

Sometime in the night, he started to growl. It was a deep growl from the back of his throat. But when I popped my eyes open, he'd already lowered his head and gone back to sleep.

## 7

### DEAD SPIDER

The next morning, I woke up early to find Treacle sitting on the kitchen counter, looking out the window.

"Good morning. See anything good out there?"

*"No."*

"Well, no news is good news, I say." I stroked his head as I walked past to the fridge to pour myself some of Bea's freshly squeezed orange juice. She'd given it to me to make sure I got my vitamins during the cold snap we were having.

*"Can I stay at Bea's today?"*

"Of course." I pouted. "You okay?"

*"I'm just a little jittery from yesterday. I'm wondering if I didn't catch something, being out in the cold so long."*

"Honey, don't say that." I stroked his head. "The

last thing either of us wants is a trip to the vet's office."

*"Tell me about it. I think some company and a little rest will do me a world of good. Peanut Butter can do all the talking. I'll listen and doze off."*

Peanut Butter was Bea's feline. He was a young cat but had proven to be an excellent familiar, and his powers, although not as strong as Treacle's yet, were well on their way.

I quickly got dressed, pulled my hair back in a sloppy ponytail, and scooped Treacle up in my arms, tucking him into the folds of my coat. It was early enough that I knew Bea hadn't left for the café yet. Plus, Jake's car was still in the driveway. What I didn't expect was for Blake to answer the door.

"What are you doing here? Did you guys have a sleepover?" I quipped as I stepped inside, then I wiped my feet and set Treacle down on the hardwood floor. He quickly trotted up to Peanut Butter for a quick hello. I watched as they absconded to the front room, where a fire was crackling in the fireplace.

"They just got home," Bea called. I followed her voice and saw Jake sitting on one of the stools at the island in the middle of Bea's kitchen while she bustled about, pouring another cup of coffee for me.

"You just got home from where?"

"Collins Funeral Home," Blake said as he placed his hands on my shoulders to move me out of his way. He motioned for me to take a seat next to Jake as he stood sipping his own cup of coffee. I climbed up on the stool and looked at Jake.

"Details."

"You won't believe this." Bea placed a bowl of dried fruits and nuts in front of me. I grabbed a handful as if it were popcorn and waited for Jake to debrief me.

"We had no idea what to expect when we walked into the funeral home," he started. "I was sure Mr. Collins was going to break down into tears as he led us to the cremation room."

"Was Mrs. Elderflower being cremated?" I asked.

"She was supposed to be. But that was all halted when we found... what we found," Blake answered.

"So, since the Elderflowers agreed they would rent the casket for the viewing, the body was—"

"Wait. They did what?" I was sure I heard this wrong.

"They rented the casket." Jake smiled as he watched the expression on my face.

"That's a real thing? You can rent a casket and put a dead body in it?"

"Of course." Blake said. "A cheap casket runs

almost six thousand dollars. The cost of a casket can easily reach ten thousand dollars if the family wants to include all the bells and whistles."

"The Elderflowers aren't rich people," Bea added. "This probably made the most sense to them."

"Gosh, I wonder how many bodies were in that casket before Marie. No chance of cross-contamination with the evidence?" I asked innocently. Jake and Blake looked at me as if I'd just tried to tell them how to wear their badges and load their weapons. "Sorry. I watched an episode of *Law & Order* the other day."

"Anyway, when Mr. Collins and his assistant went to remove the body from the casket to place her on the belt to be cremated, that was when they saw it." Jake set his coffee down and shook his head.

"Saw what?"

"Well, first, there were strange tea leaves found caught in Mrs. Elderflower's teeth and in the back of her throat. We took those to be analyzed. But then Mr. Collins discovered two of her toes had been cut off," Blake answered.

I gasped and clamped my hand over my mouth.

"That isn't all," he continued. "Whoever did this crudely hollowed out a small area in order to insert something into the cavity."

"What did they insert?" I quickly looked at Bea. "Do I want to know?"

"It was a small piece of parchment wrapped around a dead spider and a kernel of corn."

I looked at Bea, who returned my knowing glance.

"Any idea what that means?" I asked.

"Not at the moment," Blake said. "But we've got the research department looking into it."

"The research department? Good. That ought to do it. Sorry, Bea. Thanks for the oats, but I've lost my appetite. Have you guys got any leads?"

"Just one," Blake answered. "Mr. Collins said that Evelyn Elderflower was the last person to leave Marie Elderflower's body. He said they left her alone for over ten minutes and they didn't want to rush her. How do you tell a teenager that they've got to say goodbye now? That there is another family coming in to grieve their loss? It provided her with the perfect opportunity and just enough time."

I slumped as I heard this.

"Have you talked to her yet?" I asked.

"We left word with her sister Fern. She seems to be the most levelheaded at the moment."

"What was her response to your call?" Bea asked.

"Just a sigh and a promise that she'd find her

sister and bring her down as soon as possible. But she told us that Evelyn had the tendency to stay out for days at a time. But she always came back when she was hungry or cold," Blake added.

I couldn't help it. My gut was telling me this just wasn't right. I thought about that girl at the funeral. She sat next to her father with tears running down her cheeks. She looked at her mother's body. She didn't shy away or look everywhere else. She looked at the corpse in the casket without hesitation. I had to find her. From what I could see, everyone around was against her. They all had her pinned, and I thought it was only because of the way she looked. I thought that was terribly unfair. Especially since she was just a kid.

"I wonder why the older daughters didn't spring for a real casket." I let the words out without thinking.

"What do you mean?"

"Well, I heard one of them was a doctor and the other was a vet. Together, they could have probably come up with six thousand dollars. There was probably life insurance too, right?"

"If the mother wanted to be cremated, there was no reason to buy a casket," Jake said.

I shrugged. He was right about that.

"We'd better get to the café," Bea said as she pulled off her apron. "Mom is going to think we are playing hooky."

"Mind if I leave Treacle here today? He said he was feeling a little under the weather and wanted some company."

"He said he was feeling under the weather?" Blake looked at me with surprise.

I had forgotten myself. The guy was always around. He was like a permanent fixture, like a lamp or a weird candy dish.

"Of course he can stay here." Bea slid in to catch my foul. "Don't pay any attention to Cath, Blake. She loves that cat so much I swear they really can communicate." She giggled and took me by the hand as we headed toward the front door.

Bea called her I love yous and goodbyes to Jake and told them both there was food in the fridge if they got hungry before slamming the door shut behind us.

"That was close," I muttered. "What was I thinking?"

"You weren't," Bea teased. "But I don't think he's any the wiser."

"So, do you think that Evelyn did this gruesome thing to her mother's body?"

"Well, it doesn't look good for her if she was the last one with the body," Bea said. "But I have reservations."

"What are they?" I felt a wave of relief wash over me. I wasn't the only one who thought pointing the finger at Evelyn was just too convenient.

"When we were at the funeral, I didn't get a sense of malicious intent from her. There was sorrow, of course, but..."

"But what?"

"I could sense a strong hatred. Really strong."

"Are you sure it was from Evelyn? And are you sure it wasn't just a hatred for the situation and not directed at a specific person?"

"See, that's where I'm not sure. It was floating around, but for the life of me, I couldn't pinpoint it. Funeral homes can be difficult because there is so much activity at times that, for all I know, I could have been picking up on a aura that had passed through the place a week ago."

"So after all is said and done, we are really right back where we started with a whole lot of guessing and no real evidence." I didn't want to tell Bea about what Treacle had uncovered. "Maybe Marie Elderflower just died from complications due to dementia."

The wind had died down from the night before. As Bea and I walked to the café, we could see our breath through our scarves, and our shadows were crisp on the sand-colored sidewalk. Out of the corner of my eye, I thought I saw something coming up to us, but when I looked, there was nothing there.

Just before we made it to the café, I was sure someone was racing up to catch the door, but when I looked, no one was there. I shrugged it off as just the bright sun overhead playing tricks on me. It was a beautiful sunny day without a cloud in the sky. That meant the temperature would drop a little more. Sunny days were always the coldest. Funny how something so pleasant-looking could be the most dangerous.

fter opening the café and serving the handful of patrons who stopped in before work, Bea and I filled in Aunt Astrid on everything Jake and Blake had told us. She listened intently. When we finished, Bea and I stood back, folded our arms, and waited.

"So," I piped up. "What should we do?"

"The first thing we need to do is find out what the ritual is that cuts off toes and leaves things inside the space," Aunt Astrid suggested. "I have a book, the *Rites of the Dead*, down in the bunker."

"I'll go get it," Bea offered and trotted off to the practically invisible door that led to our secret plotting, planning, and scheming room.

We'd had no idea the room was even there. Had the Brew-Ha-Ha not almost burned to the ground a while back, it would still be hidden. Now, it was adorned with a pretty area rug, a fridge, snacks, tea, and several of Aunt Astrid's favorite "cookbooks."

Just as Bea yelled that she found the book, the tinkling of bells went off. I turned around to see none other than Evelyn Elderflower. She was standing there with another person in equally gothic attire. The handful of customers stared at them.

"Hi," I said happily. "Evelyn, right?"

She nodded and fought not to smile too brightly.

"Have a seat, honey. Would you guys like some coffee?"

Again, Evelyn nodded without saying anything. She and her friend snuck to a quiet table for two in the corner away from the window. Everyone's eyes were on them until they sat down and started whispering, as young ladies their age always did.

I filled two cups and brought them over, making sure not to treat the girls as if they were girls but rather paying customers I'd seen a million times.

"I'm glad you stopped in," I said as I placed the cups in front of them.

"It doesn't look like your customers are," Evelyn snapped, looking at everyone who had turned to look at her and sticking out her tongue.

"I think they'll all survive your visit. You guys want something to eat?"

They both declined, but I wanted to get them to stay as long as possible. Like luring a scared dog that had seen the crueler side of humans, I went to the counter and picked out a couple of things for them to share. One thing teenagers rarely turned down was food. Especially sweets.

"Here. Try these." I set down a plate filled with brownie bites, two blueberry muffins, and some sliced honey crisp apples.

"Um, we don't have any money for this," Evelyn whispered. She looked at her friend with embarrassment.

"It's on the house," I whispered back.

That was it. That was all it took. There it was. A smile.

"Can you stay for a little while? I'd like to talk to you."

Taking a big bite of blueberry muffin, Evelyn nodded.

I walked back behind the counter and made sure that Evelyn could see I wasn't talking about her to Aunt Astrid. When Bea came up with the book, she saw Evelyn chatting with her friend and immediately went toward the phone.

"What are you doing?" I asked.

"Calling Jake to tell him Evelyn Elderflower is here."

"No, you're not." I gently took the phone from her hand and put it back on the cradle.

"Why?" she asked. "You heard him this morning. He wants to talk to her about what she did."

"Do you really think she did that?" I asked quietly.

Bea looked from me to Evelyn and back again. She picked up the coffee pot and made the rounds. When she got to Evelyn and her friend, she placed a hand on Evelyn's shoulder.

"Are you warming up? It's bitter cold out there," Bea said pleasantly.

"I think it'll take a little longer for my toes to thaw," her friend said.

"Yeah, combat boots look warm, but I think these were made for the desert," Evelyn said as she showed Bea her clunky footwear.

Bea chuckled and came back to the counter.

"So?" I asked as I folded more Valentine's napkins for our to-go customers.

"There's nothing there." Bea was trembling.

"What do you mean?"

"Either that girl has not a single emotion inside

her, or someone or something is preventing me from observing it." Bea nervously bit her bottom lip.

"Are you saying she's like a sociopath?" I asked.

"No. Even they have some kind of aura. I'm saying this little girl is in trouble either by her own hand or by the hand of someone else. I'm afraid she's opened a door to something she doesn't understand and it's hurting her without her even knowing. I've got to call Jake."

"Don't do that." Aunt Astrid stood up from her table and pushed herself past us to grab a glass and the pitcher of water. "We've got bigger issues to address."

Neither Bea nor I knew what Aunt Astrid was talking about until we turned around.

"There you are!" It was Fern and Gail Elderflower. They were fit to be tied. "Get your coat on! We're leaving!"

"Excuse me, ladies." Aunt Astrid quickly placed her body between the sisters and Evelyn. "Is there a problem? Normally, people don't come into the café, yelling."

"Well, normally, we don't have the police looking for our delinquent sister, but this morning, we do," Gail snapped at Aunt Astrid.

I looked at Evelyn. All the pale makeup in the

world couldn't hide the humiliation she was feeling. Her cheeks were bright red. Her eyes were beginning to fill with tears as she stood from the table.

"Don't start with the waterworks," Gail ordered. "It isn't going to work."

"Just get your coat and get in the car," Fern added.

"Why don't you ladies calm down and have a cup of tea." Bea reached out to touch Fern but soon regretted it.

"Don't touch me!" she hissed. "I don't know who you are, but this is a family matter! Evelyn, let's move!"

Thrusting her hands deep in the pockets of her long black coat, Evelyn stared down at the floor. She pushed past Aunt Astrid and her sisters. Her friend meekly got up to leave too.

Evelyn's push against the door was so hard I gasped for fear it would break. We'd just gotten it fixed after the giant hairless cat of Christmas attacked. But that was a story for another time.

Aunt Astrid stared at the Elderflower girls. I tried to see what she was seeing, but something big moved out of the corner of my eye. When I looked, there was nothing there. When I looked back, the sisters were staring at me.

"Care for some coffee to go?" I said.

"Look, our sister is nothing but trouble. You obviously think that's cute. Well, you'll learn soon enough when she brings you nothing but trouble. Mark my words. You'll learn soon enough."

They stomped out of the café like soldiers looking for a traitor.

The people in the café let out their breaths and began talking about the scene that had just unfolded.

I looked at my aunt and cousin. "What do you think of that?" I asked.

"I think we have a bigger problem than we thought," Aunt Astrid said quietly as she began stacking her receipts. "You were right, Cath. It's not Evelyn at all."

"Really? You don't think so?" I sighed as I walked over to the table the two girls were at and began to clean up. That was when I found it. A note. Quickly, I brought it over to Bea and my aunt.

"Meet me at the Night Owl Café tonight. Midnight. E.E."

"Did she write that before or after her sisters arrived?" Bea asked.

"I bet after," I said.

"How is she going to meet you if they take her to

the police and Jake holds her? He won't let us talk to her there. It could get him in trouble."

"I have a feeling Evelyn has slipped away from her sisters more than once. She's probably planning on doing the same thing again," I replied.

I was never so excited for midnight to come in my life. The only bad thing was that Tom had decided to come by after his seven-to-eleven shift.

"You're going to the Night Owl Café to meet someone?" He looked suspicious and hurt. "Why?"

"Because the person asked me to. It's that simple," I said as I wrapped my scarf around my neck a couple times.

"And why can't I go with you?"

"Because it will look suspicious," I answered plainly.

"To whom?"

I stopped before swinging my coat around to slip my arms inside.

"Do you think I'm going to meet a dude?" I asked.

Tom shrugged and stuffed his hands into his front jeans pockets.

"I'm flattered you think anyone else would be interested in me. But I think you are the only one with enough brain damage to want to hitch your wagon to my star."

"Then you don't mind if I come with you?" He took a step closer. After all the things Tom had been through with me, there was no way I could say no now. He accepted my family and me and everything that came with it.

"If it will put your mind at ease," I said, stepping a little closer to him. "But would you mind staying in the car while I go in?"

"Why?"

"If she sees a cop with me, she might freak."

"Whoever this is doesn't want to see any police? Cath, is this person dangerous?"

"That's the thing. Everyone thinks she is, but she's not. She's just a kid." I swallowed hard. "It's Evelyn Elderflower. She needs my help."

Tom looked surprised. He stepped forward and took hold of the lapels of my coat. With his thumb, he brushed over the bright-green brooch that was there.

"Then let's go help her."

## ❧ 9 ❧

## GONE AGAIN

The Night Owl Café was reviewed in the local paper as a rustic lounge with books along the walls. The novels, ranging from *The Tropic of Capricorn* to *Fifty Shades of Grey*, were for the patrons to read at their leisure while sipping hot coffee or tea. It used to be known for a fantastic shepherd's pie, but an entrepreneur who catered to the younger crowd bought the place and made it much more rustic compared to the Brew-Ha-Ha. Food selections were now limited to frozen pizza or ramen noodles. Cheap eats were an attraction for the high school and college crowds. Open poetry nights were also a crowd pleaser.

"This is like a dirtier, slummy version of the Brew-Ha-Ha." Tom winced as he pulled his truck up to the curb. "Are you sure you don't want me to go with you?"

"At this hour, there are mostly college kids inside. It's not a biker bar. I'll be all right," I said as I unclicked my seat belt.

"How long am I supposed to sit here all by myself?"

"I won't be long. I promise." I kissed Tom's cheek then climbed out of his truck. I could hear experimental jazz music coming from inside. As soon as I pulled the door open, I was hit by the smell of patchouli and pizza.

As much as I hated the competition, I couldn't help but admire the elaborate lights hanging from the ceiling. They looked as though they'd been snagged from the set of some Dario Argento film. Rich red, green and yellow vintage swag hanging lights gave the place a soft, soothing glow.

Bulky velvet couches and armchairs filled the floor. A bar stretched across the far-right wall, where patrons sat on mismatched bar stools, sipping their java. Coffee tables and end tables also had thrift-store lamps on them, and there were worn-out Persian rugs on the floor. Bookshelves lined the walls. From where I was standing, I could see the categories written on pieces of cardstock that had long ago started to curl at the edges. Fiction. Nonfiction. History. Current Events. Sci-fi. Romance. All the usual suspects, along with a few exotics like an entire section of Idiot's Guides and another of encyclopedias from the 1970s. Of course, there was an extensive occult section. I shuddered to think of what nonsense was being passed around in the books here. Before I could go peruse the titles, I saw a familiar pale face. Evelyn Elderflower waved to me. Her nails were black, and she had huge clunky rings on each finger.

"How did you manage to get away from your sisters?" I asked. I had to maneuver around a huge, cushy loveseat with two Goth kids sitting in it. They looked at me the same way everyone at the Brew-Ha-ha had looked at Evelyn that morning.

"It wasn't easy." She scooted over and made room for me on the couch.

"Do you want to go somewhere to talk?" I asked.

"Why? What's wrong with this place?" Her attitude was starting to creep up.

"Not a thing. So, what did you want to talk to me about?"

She nervously looked around.

"Evelyn, you're safe with me here."

"Ha." She snickered, blowing smoke from her nostrils. "You don't see them, do you?"

"See who?"

She shook her head, making her long black hair wave across her face.

"My mother."

"You can see your mother?" I was surprised to say the least.

"No, stupid." She snickered. "I'm trying to tell you about my mother. Everyone thinks she was a mental case. They say she had dementia or suffered from schizophrenia. My mother was as sane as you and me sitting here."

It felt as if I were treading on thin ice. Should I tell Evelyn what I had heard from Aunt Astrid about Marie Elderflower? Was it smart to tell her anything about what Jake and Blake had said? This was one of those rare occasions I decided to keep my mouth closed.

"I know what you're thinking," she continued. "You've heard the stories about the cops coming to the house and my mom getting violent. Traipsing around in the backyard in the middle of the night. Her obsession with lights and candles."

"I'm sorry, Evelyn. I don't really know anything about your family," I answered quietly, as if I were talking to a little bird that might fly away with any sudden movements. "My aunt knew your mom a little. She said they met at the library and had a lot in common. She said your mother had a wonderful sense of humor."

That was all I could think of to say. I hoped it would be enough to get her to continue talking.

"Well, if you check the police blotter from over the past year, you'll see how many times the police were called to the house. We were on our way to becoming *that* family. You know, the house the kids don't go trick-or-treating at because crazy old Mrs. Elderflower will definitely put razor blades in the apples.

"People are supposed to be safe in their homes. I tried to help. I really did. I thought if I got between her and him that it would all stop. But my mom was stronger than me. The one time she pushed me, I fell down the basement stairs. All I could think was that she was going to shut the door and lock me in. I'd be forced to hear what was going on upstairs."

Had I totally misread this whole situation? Was this a case of child abuse and not something paranormal? For a few more seconds, Evelyn continued looking straight ahead. Then she looked at me, grinning. I wondered if she wasn't telling a big, long fairy story to see if I'd bite.

"Was your father there?"

"Sometimes. But he wasn't much help. Like now. He can't do anything."

"Is this why you did that thing to your mother's body at the funeral home?"

Evelyn tilted her head to the right. "Did what thing?"

The look in her eyes told me she had no idea what I was talking about. I wasn't sure which one of us was more confused.

"Evelyn, I don't know if I'm understanding you right. Did your mother beat you? Or was it your father?"

"Ha!" She smacked her lips as if I'd said something offensive. "Well, that's how it looks, right? And who would believe me? Look at me. Evil Evelyn Elderflower. Anything that comes out of my mouth must be a lie."

"I didn't say that at all." The time for tiptoeing around was over. "Look, you called me here, and here I am. But if you want my help, and I think you do, you need to quit with this Morticia act and just tell me what you want me to know."

Had I gone too far? Was I going to be added to the list of adults she thought she couldn't trust?

Evelyn swallowed hard and blinked.

"You won't believe me, Cath, because I don't believe it myself." She finished her cigarette and stamped it out in the massive orange speckled ashtray from the 1960s that sat on the coffee table in front of us.

"You'd be surprised at what I might believe, Evelyn. I happen to know for a fact that monsters lived under my bed."

What made me open up to Evelyn like that, I couldn't say. But the relief I saw on her face nearly moved me to tears. Her bottom lip trembled as if she was afraid to say anything else but desperately wanted to. After a few seconds, I was crossing my fingers that she'd explain further, but it was no use. The door was open a crack, but it wasn't going any farther.

"My sisters. They don't like people like you," Evelyn said.

"People like me?" A million thoughts went through my head. What was she talking about?

Short people? People who worked in coffee shops? Brunettes? I didn't understand at all.

There was a shadow that fell over the coffee table as though someone were rushing up to us. When I turned to look, there was nothing there. I chalked it up to a trick of the lights. But the look on Evelyn's face terrified me.

"Evelyn? Honey? Are you all right?"

"You better go."

"Why? Honey, we can talk for as long as you like."

"No, Cath. You really better get going." Evelyn stood up. She had a cute figure, and it was obvious that the boys, Goth or not, took notice of her. She didn't seem to see any of them. That was also odd behavior for a girl her age. She reminded me of Aunt Astrid, who would stare like that. But Aunt Astrid could see another dimension. Could Evelyn see that too?

"Wait, Evelyn."

The girl scooted from behind the coffee table and began to head for the back door. I followed her, but she stopped me quickly.

"Don't follow me," she whispered. "Promise you won't."

"Evelyn, my boyfriend is outside in his truck. Let

us drive you home. It's cold outside, and it's very late. Please."

"I can get home myself." Her head didn't move, but her eyes were scanning the periphery as if she were waiting for something. Suddenly, I was starting to feel nervous. Was this a setup? She wasn't going to have some of her Goth goons jump me in the parking lot, was she?

"Evelyn. Will you come by the café? The back door to the kitchen is almost always open. You can get in that way, and you'll be safe there."

"I'm not safe anywhere."

Before I could grab hold of her arm, she was gone down a short hallway and out the back door of the Night Owl Café.

I got the feeling someone was staring at me from behind. When I whirled around, I saw Tom.

"She's gone again?"

"Yeah." I slipped my hand in his. "I know I might be asking you to break the copper code, but could you not tell anyone I met her here? She's not going anywhere. She's got no way to skip town. A few more days, and I bet she comes around on her own."

"She's not in my jurisdiction. I'm not violating any copper code," Tom assured me. "Come on. Let's get home."

After Tom dropped me off at my house, I instantly tore off all my clothes to get them washed immediately and showered to get the cigarette smell out of my hair.

"*Don't go down there at this hour,*" Treacle scolded. "*That stuff can wait until morning.*"

"Are you kidding? My whole house will reek of cigarettes if I don't," I said. "It's funny. I don't mind the smell of cigarettes in a place like the Night Owl Café, but in my house, ugh. It makes me want to hurl."

"*Then just throw the stuff down there and wash it tomorrow.*"

"What is the matter with you, Treacle? We've done laundry at two in the morning before. Why shouldn't we do it now?"

I watched my cat look from me to the basement door and back to me again.

"*Fine. If you insist. But I'm going down there first.*"

"Fine. Go down there first. I don't care who goes first. It's not a race. Just some laundry. Sheesh."

I didn't pay too much attention to Treacle as I opened the basement door. The familiar smell of dampness and concrete filled my nose. I didn't hear any weird noises. The light from the kitchen illuminated the first few steps, where I always kept my flashlight.

"I wonder what the motivation was to put the light switch all the way on the other side of the basement," I said and got no reply. "Treacle, could we move along? This isn't a modeling runway."

"*Shhh,*" he hissed back.

Something had obviously gotten his tail in a spin.

There was a cold breeze cutting through the heat from the furnace. The window Treacle would come in and out of was still open.

"*You didn't close that?*"

"No, honey. How are you going to come and go if I don't leave that cracked? We'll lock it up tight when the rainy season starts in a few weeks. Okay?"

Treacle didn't reply.

"You want me to close it?"

"*Yes.*" He didn't give me a reason but looked at me with his green eyes wide.

"Fine. I'll close it. But if you get stuck in the cold, don't complain to me."

Finally, with my feet on solid concrete, I padded across the floor. The light from the flashlight bobbed up and down. I slapped the window shut and turned the small latch to lock it. Once at the light switch, I flicked it on and saw something swoop out of the corner of my eye.

Treacle's back was arched, and his fur was up like porcupine quills. Within seconds, he shrank back to normal size and shook his head.

"Boy, those shadows sure can play tricks on you," I said as I dropped the smelly clothes in the washer. After adding all the detergent and softener, I set the washing machine in motion and was about to flip off the overhead light when Treacle stopped me.

*"You may as well leave the light on. You're going to have to come down here again to put things in the dryer."*

"Good point," I agreed and was a good bit thankful. Something about the dark tonight didn't sit well with me. Plus, I was very vulnerable in my underwear. "Let's go. I've got to get this smell out of my hair."

Normally, on cold days like this, I enjoyed a long, hot shower. But something didn't feel right. Perhaps it was that Evelyn had left in such a hurry, leaving so many unanswered questions. Maybe it was that I felt guilty for not making her come with me. I even thought I felt a little remorse for not telling Jake and Blake I knew where she was. But this was something different. I was out of the shower and bundled up in sweatpants, a sweatshirt, and my fuzzy socks within five minutes.

"Does my hair smell back to normal?" I asked Treacle.

He crawled up to my face on the pillow and gave me a headbutt.

*"Yeah."*

"I think the temperature is supposed to be a little warmer tomorrow. You want me to open the window downstairs again or keep it shut?"

*"Let's play it by ear."* He nuzzled me before heading to the end of the bed.

My body felt tired, but my mind was on fast-forward. I couldn't unwind, no matter how hard I tried. It was three o'clock in the morning when I turned on the light on my nightstand and climbed out of bed.

The air in my house was perfectly cool for sleeping but not for being up and walking the floors. With a few taps of the thermostat, I got the heat going.

After a drink of water and a peek outside the front-room window, I came back to bed to find Treacle standing on the edge of the bed, puffed up and ready to pounce.

"What is it?"

*"In the corner. See it?"*

There was no reason for me to think it was anything other than a mouse. They were all over this time of year, trying to escape the cold.

I squinted in the direction Treacle was looking. From deep inside his throat, I heard the menacing growl of a feline ready for a fight. He didn't do that when he saw a mouse. In fact, he was stealthy and silent as he crept up on any of his prey.

Whatever was there, I didn't want to scare away. So I got down on my hands and knees on the floor next to Treacle and tried to focus.

"I don't see anything. Are you sure there is—"

My words caught in my throat as the red eye blinked at me. I froze.

*"See it now?"*

"I see something. Is that a rat?"

Mice were bad enough. Gross little pooping machines that left a trail of excrement wherever they went. Just because I could talk to most animals didn't mean I liked all of them. But rats? A rat in my house terrified me. They were as mean and dirty as they were portrayed in the movies.

*"Not a rat,"* Treacle growled.

I slowly stood up and stepped cautiously over to

the light switch and flipped it on. There was nothing there.

"Wait. I saw a red eye. Did you see a red eye?"

Treacle looked at me then back at the corner.

Neither of us slept. Not until the horizon turned from black to a rich cobalt blue. There was nothing to be afraid of as long as the sun was coming up. At least, that was what we thought. We later learned that wasn't necessarily true.

# PAYMENT PLAN

"That poor girl," Bea said after I told her and Aunt Astrid about my late-night discussion with Evelyn Elderflower. "I wonder if that could be what's covering her aura."

We had just opened the café. With the temperature a balmy forty-something, we had quite a bit of foot traffic. It took me over an hour to get all the details out. After I repeated the strange things Evelyn had said, I felt even worse for her.

"Does that happen? Do victims of child abuse cover their auras?" I asked.

"Your guess is as good as mine. I'm really just thinking out loud." Bea looked at her mother.

"Well, after we talked, she got spooked by something," I continued. "Before I could stop her, she left the Night Owl through the back door, and that was the end of that. I don't know. Bea, Aunt Astrid, should I have called Jake? I'm feeling guilty about not getting him involved."

"Don't be too hard on yourself," Bea said soothingly. "Jake was at the station around that time last night. When he got home this morning, he told me that Evelyn had come in by herself."

I gasped. "You're kidding! I didn't see that coming."

"What did she tell Jake?" Aunt Astrid asked as she fixed herself a cup of tea.

"According to him, she had that typical teenage rebellious attitude. But he did say when he described what was done to her mother's body, she went ghostly pale."

"Did she have any idea that it had happened?"

"Jake isn't sure. Of course, he played the jail-time card. He told her the penalty for desecrating a body was up to eight years in prison plus a fine. How would she like it if her sisters had to pay that for her? Did she want something like that on her record? You know the routine."

When my aunt asked what Evelyn's response was, I could see she was searching for something in addition to her verbal answer.

"Jake said she had tears in her eyes but she

denied having anything to do with it. Then she asked him if she was being charged. She's no dummy," Bea replied.

"If they weren't charging her, she didn't have to answer any more questions." I felt relieved the girl was smart enough to know that. "What did Jake think after he was done talking to her? And was Blake there? That guy's got an opinion on everything. What was his take?"

"He said he thought she was either feeling remorseful or covering for someone. Of course, he was leaning toward remorse."

"Tears," Aunt Astrid muttered. "That's a good sign. The girl isn't lost."

Bea and I asked what she meant by that.

"I was doing a little reading myself last night. I wanted to know what the dead spider and the kernel of corn were all about. We all forgot about the *Rites of the Dead* after the spectacle with the Elderflower sisters."

I slapped my head.

"I forgot," Bea said.

"It's a good thing I didn't." My aunt looked around to make sure no one would hear what we were saying. "The book stated that this was part of a payment plan of sorts."

"A payment plan?" I picked up one of the red paper napkins and began worrying it. "Like for a car?"

"More like for a favor. Think Gazzo in the movie *Rocky*."

Bea and I looked at my aunt blankly.

"The loan shark Rocky worked for. This severed toe and the insertion of a dead spider and a corn kernel were payment for a favor. However, according to the book, it was a first payment. There are more to follow."

"So, what you're saying is that Evelyn is somehow tied to a paranormal loan shark. What does he want next? Her kneecaps? Maybe her thumbs?" I scratched my head.

"Why on earth would Evelyn owe a debt like this?" Bea asked.

"You tell me. My guess is that she dove into the occult business with her eyes wide shut. She messed around with a Ouija board, tried some random spells —you know how kids her age want to be special. I'm thinking she accidentally set the wheels in motion for a very dangerous scenario."

"But she said she didn't know anything about it. Something in my gut tells me she's telling the truth," I argued.

"That doesn't change the fact that this Gazzo is going to come looking for his next payment. If she doesn't have it, I'm afraid the consequences will be worse than she ever imagined." My aunt sipped her tea.

"So what can we do?" Bea asked.

"I'm working on that," Aunt Astrid assured us.

But I still felt as if there was a big piece of the story missing. Sure, Evelyn could have dabbled in something she shouldn't have. But how? Tarots and Ouija boards didn't hook the living up with paranormal mobsters by accident. I had a feeling this was a deliberate action.

"But where would she have gotten the information?" I mumbled. "I'm going to take a stroll over to the Elderflowers' house."

"No, you are not," Bea said. "Not until we have a better grasp on what's going on."

"Yes, I am. Evelyn wanted to talk to me yesterday. Not Jake. Not you guys. Me. If I can get a look in her room, maybe I can find out how she made contact with this Gazzo, and we'll have an easier time getting her out of this contract."

"How are you going to get in?" Aunt Astrid asked.

"The same way you guys did. I'll bring a care package."

"All the same. Don't go until Bea and I can get you a proper protection spell. No use you getting hurt in the process."

I agreed to wait until closing time. That turned out to be perfect since once I arrived in my beat-up car on the Elderflowers' block, I saw Fern and Gail outside with their father. They were going somewhere. Either the house was empty, or Evelyn was alone. Either option worked for me.

## ❧ 11 ❧

## AS QUIET AS A TOMB

O nce the Elderflowers' car had driven out of sight, I parked my car a few doors down. With a pastry box filled with poppy-seed muffins, I trotted up to the front door and knocked. There was no answer. I rang the bell. Still nothing.

Just about every curtain was drawn over the windows facing the street. I looked around but didn't see anyone else outside. *Of course* no one else was outside. It was chilly, and the sky was covered with cold, gray clouds. I was the only one around.

Acting as though I did it all the time, I skipped off the front step and trotted around to the back of the house. Keeping it professional, I knocked on the back door. If I stood on my tiptoes, I could look in the kitchen window.

"As quiet as a tomb," I said. Now the only problem would be getting into the house. How was I going to pull that off? I stepped back and looked at what I had to work with.

The Elderflowers lived in an older tri-level house. The style itself was timeless, but the Elderflowers had left some telltale retro details in place that made the house look old. It was brick with siding that was painted olive green. It totally complemented the orange front door. At least, it had in 1971.

The windows were a variety of shapes and sizes. The driveway was in desperate need of tarring. There were a few evergreen bushes along the front and side of the house. Some of them had grown out of control after not being trimmed for some time. Those that didn't were crispy, dry, and reddish-brown.

As I slunk around, I thought about what Evelyn had said that people were supposed to feel safe at home. When she looked at this place, she saw where she'd grown up. Not the dead bushes and outdated color scheme. Somewhere along the line, it had ceased to be a refuge and became her prison.

I reached for the doorknob on the back door. Locked.

"Of course," I mumbled. "There's got to be a way to get in." I was an inch away from taking a rock and smashing one of the basement windows when an opportunity presented itself. As I circled around the house, I noticed that behind one of the dead bushes, the garage had a tall window covered not by glass but by decorative gold-colored plastic. It was cracked right down the middle.

"It's going to require a smidge of vandalism, Cath. Are you sure you want to do it?" The truth was that the plastic was easily going to crack out of its old window molding sometime within the next six months. Maybe a year. I was just helping it along.

There was no time to waste hemming and hawing about the ethics of the situation. I pushed the plastic, and as I'd hoped, with the cold weather, it snapped right up the middle and came out in my hand.

Inhaling deeply, I squeezed through the window and was in the garage. I propped the plastic back in place, happy that it looked almost the same as it had before I damaged it.

I crossed the garage to the door that led into the house. Pressing my ear up against the cold wood, I listened. The only thing I could hear was my heartbeat in my ears. It sounded like a raging river.

Carefully, I turned the doorknob and pushed the door open. Still, I heard nothing but the tick of a clock and the hum of the furnace going. I shut the door behind me and let out my breath.

"You're in. You just wanted to check out Evelyn's room. Don't waste time snooping around the other rooms. You still need to get out unseen."

I walked a few paces, and on my right were the stairs. With the first step, I set off an alarm of creaks and groans from the worn-out steps. I knew every house-settling sound in my own home. If anyone were around, they'd know immediately there was a trespasser in their midst. I held my breath. Still no movement.

"You're alone, Cath. Let's get this accomplished."

With a bit more reckless abandon, I took the stairs two at a time. Once on the landing, I carefully looked in the rooms. A king-size bed, matching dresser with a mirror attached to it, and a wedding picture of Marie Elderflower and Mr. Elderflower hanging on the wall told me this was their room. A small bathroom was next on the left. Across from it was a locked room. At the end of the hallway was another closed door. But when I turned the knob, it opened. Slowly, I pushed my way in. It was Evelyn's room. Quickly, I shut the door behind me.

I had expected black walls, posters of Marilyn Manson or The Misfits, candles, some skulls, a makeshift Wiccan altar, or something like that. Instead, the walls were lavender. The bed was neatly made with a leopard-print comforter. On the night-stand was the picture of a smiling Evelyn standing between her mother and father. A dartboard against the wall had more pictures of her with her parents, friends from school, and the girl who had been with her at the café. There were ticket stubs to a ballet, an opera, and the symphony.

"This is weird." It seemed that Evelyn was a bit more cultured than she appeared at first sight. It got even more bizarre when I looked at the books on her bookshelves.

There was no *Satanic Bible*. No *Wicca & Witchcraft for Dummies*. Instead, there were an overwhelming number of Victorian romance novels on the shelves. Sure, I saw a few Stephen King novels and two books on haunted places throughout the state. But none of this made an occultist.

"Well, I don't know what to think about any of this. I'm stumped."

I sat down on her bed for a moment. It squeaked loudly, sending a ripple up my spine. I held my breath and waited. Nothing. No sound of pounding feet heading in my direction.

It was the logical next step. I looked underneath

her bed. I opened the closet. Aside from half a dozen black blouses and skirts, there were, surprisingly, a lot of colorful garments hanging there.

"She doesn't fit the Goth profile at all. What is going on?"

I went to her dresser and pulled open the top drawer. In addition to socks and underwear was a pretty diary.

I picked it up and looked at the cover. On a black backdrop, a shimmering goldfish with long elegant fins swam through the darkness. It was pretty.

"And it's private, Cath. You can't."

I held it in my hand for what felt like an hour, turning it over and over, contemplating whether I should read what was inside or not. A million reasons whispered through my head. She could be in danger. She could be suicidal. She could be ready to hurt someone else. Finally, I thought the reasons to read it outweighed the girl's right to privacy.

The last entry was the day after her mother had passed. It was short and chilling.

*One down. Two to go.*

Before I could backtrack and read anything from an earlier date, I heard the stairs groan. It was the same sound they made when I stepped on them. My entire body went ice cold.

*What do I do?*

First, I shut the bedroom door.

I quickly put the diary back where I found it. Then I looked toward the window. It was always a bad idea to put a teenager's room next to a big, sturdy tree with welcoming branches. How many times had Evelyn snuck out this way to meet her friends?

Now it was my turn.

I raised the window but winced as it scraped in its old pane. If whoever was down the stairs thought they were mistaken, that sound confirmed they had an intruder. Without waiting I swung one leg out the window and placed it firmly on the thick branch. I looked toward the door to see the doorknob turning.

Something inside welled up, and I felt the urge to scream. Instead, I bit my tongue. The door never swung open. I didn't face the angry faces of the Elderflower family. Instead, it stopped turning, and I saw something I couldn't explain.

On the floor, something appeared to be seeping into Evelyn's room. A dark thing that rushed forward then receded like a tiny black tide. It rolled into the room three or four inches before it disappeared back underneath the crack again, moving like a liquid but leaving nothing wet on the floor in its wake.

I couldn't be sure it was anything but a trick of the lighting. Was someone moving on the other side of the door, casting shadows on the floor? But why did these shadows appear to reach like long fingers? Why didn't I hear anyone on the other side of that door? And if they knew I was here, why didn't they come bursting in to catch me?

There was no way I was going to wait for a logical answer to any of these questions. With the speed and agility to rival any teenager, I swung my other leg out the window, holding tightly to a thinner branch overhead. With the grace of a drunk on New Year's Eve, I wobbled my way to the trunk of the tree and climbed down, the branches scraping my face and hands and tearing my jeans, and getting sap in my hair in the process.

My first instinct when my feet finally hit solid ground was to bolt to my car. But I looked up. When I did, I saw Evelyn's curtains fluttering and the silhouette of someone standing behind them. It was a dark figure. I didn't know which of the Elder-flowers it might have been. But the heat of their stare sent me tumbling out of there.

When I finally reached my car, I dove inside,

locked the doors, started the engine, and cranked up the heat. My whole body was trembling as I made a U-turn on the street. I didn't want to drive past the house. I didn't want whoever was in there to see my car. Although I was pretty sure they got a good glimpse of my face.

"But who was it?" The words just tumbled out of my mouth as the heat began to penetrate my frozen limbs. "Gail, Fern, and their father left. You saw them. It wasn't Evelyn. She wouldn't have tried to scare you even if she did see you reading her diary. Plus, that figure was too big. Too masculine."

I shivered at the thought.

When I finally got back to the café, I wasn't sure what to tell Aunt Astrid and Bea. So I sat down at the counter and spilled the beans.

"Are you sure you were alone in the house?" Aunt Astrid asked.

"Pretty sure," I replied as Bea poured me a cup of tea. "I didn't go looking through the whole house. I was focused on Evelyn's room. I figured that would be where she kept her occult stuff."

"But there wasn't anything?" Bea asked.

"It was a really pretty little girl's room. Nothing menacing. There was nothing that would lead her on the path to possession. If she invited some kind of

Gazzo into her house, I couldn't find proof. However, there was one thing."

I repeated the words I'd read in her diary.

Neither Aunt Astrid nor Bea said anything.

"That doesn't sound good." Bea finally spoke after cutting a piece of carrot cake for a customer and placing it on a tiny white plate.

"I'll take that. What table?" I asked.

Bea pointed to a man sitting and reading the paper by the window. I gave him his cake, and he smiled pleasantly before digging in. When I looked out the window, I thought I saw someone standing there, but the light was just playing tricks on me. It was a normal cloudy day. Cars were driving by. People bundled up against the chill walked past the café. For a second, I was back in the normal world. But then I saw something else out of the corner of my eye. When I looked, there was nothing there.

"Aunt Astrid, have you been seeing an influx of 'visitors' lately?" I used my fingers to emphasize that I was talking about the paranormal kind. "I keep seeing things moving out of the corners of my eyes. When I look, bubkes."

"Maybe it's your radar of love." Bea smirked then nodded toward the window.

Tom stood there holding a bouquet of flowers.

As crazy as it might seem, I let Evelyn and the Elderflower house slip from my mind. Partially because I needed a break. But I also didn't want to talk to my police-officer boyfriend about breaking and entering a home in search of occult paraphernalia.

"What are you doing here?" I asked.

"I came to see you and bring you these." He handed me the flowers.

"Valentine's Day isn't for almost another week."

"Are you kidding? I'm not doing this because it's Valentine's Day. I'm just doing it because you are my favorite girl. That's all."

"That's so sweet," Bea teased. "You guys should get matching shirts that say 'I'm his' and 'I'm hers' and wear them out for dinner."

"Hey, that's a great idea!" Tom replied with wide eyes and a huge grin.

"You guys are both nuts," I said.

Aunt Astrid chuckled as she counted her receipts and took a sip of tea.

"You want to join me for dinner tonight?" he asked after taking a seat at the counter. "I was thinking we could make some spaghetti at your house. I think *Casablanca* is on the classic movie channel. Or maybe it's *The African Queen*. I can't remember, but I know it's a Humphrey Bogart movie."

The idea of staying inside my own warm house with everything being familiar and cozy sounded wonderful.

"Great. I'll bring all the supplies. You just have the television on and some hot chocolate on the stove." Tom kissed my cheek, but his hand found the curve in my waist, and he pulled me to him tightly. It was just a second. No one even noticed. But my heart raced, and heat from my feet darted up my body to flood my cheeks.

"You really have yourself a great guy, Cath," Aunt Astrid said as she rooted around under the counter before pulling out a vase for my flowers.

"Yeah, he's okay," I replied.

"You are as crazy about him as he is about you. Don't think you are fooling anyone with that tough-guy act," Bea said, smiling as she handed some change back to a woman wearing a giant heart pin on the lapel of her coat.

"Speaking of tough guys, what are you getting Jake for Valentine's Day?" I quickly changed the focus from me to Bea.

"I've got a special menu I'm cooking up for him

and bringing to work for us to have a picnic in his office."

"Is it tofu? Nothing says 'I love you' like tofu," I teased.

"No. It's not tofu. It's his favorite. Vegetarian chili with corn bread and apple pie for dessert," Bea replied and stuck her tongue out at me.

"How come no one is asking me what I'm doing for Valentine's Day?" my aunt interrupted.

Bea and I looked at each other. I didn't hide my surprise. My mouth hung open like a largemouth bass's.

"What are you doing for Valentine's Day, Mom?"

"I am having dinner at my house," she replied proudly.

"With whom?" I asked.

"Blake." She giggled.

"Detective Blake Samberg? Jake's partner? You are having a Valentine's Day dinner with the Scrooge of all seasons?" I looked at Bea. It was her turn to do an impression of a largemouth bass.

"You girls need to calm down. We are having a meal together on a day when we tell people how much we love them. Just like I love you girls and I love Jake. I love Blake because, whether you like him or not, he helps keep Jake safe. To me, that is what family does. We keep each other safe."

I looked at Bea and wrinkled my nose. She was about to cry.

"Pull yourself together, Bea." I patted her shoulder.

"I just never thought of that. But Mom is right. She's totally right. Maybe we should do something nice for Blake too."

"Right. Because all the free coffee and sandwiches and salads and desserts just don't say thanks enough." I rolled my eyes.

Of course, I felt the same way Bea did. I just didn't want anyone to know it. Blake was a good guy. He did look out for Jake as if they were brothers. But I was moving ahead. I couldn't see him as anything more than a friend of the family. Maybe I could muster up enough affection for him as a second cousin or perhaps a great-uncle by marriage. But anything more might risk resurrecting those old feelings. That was something I didn't want to happen.

"He knows we don't want anything to happen to him." I turned to face my aunt. "I hope you guys have a really nice time. What are you cooking?"

I hoped it was a meat-and-potatoes meal. He liked those.

## THE BLACKNESS

"Cath, the movie is starting," Tom called from my living room.

"I'm coming," I said as I balanced a basket of garlic bread in my arms while carrying two glasses of pink lemonade. "So which one is it? *Casablanca* or *The African Queen?*"

"I was totally wrong. It's actually *Hush, Hush, Sweet Charlotte.*"

"How do you even make that mistake?" I teased as I sank down carefully onto my couch, then I set the glasses down on the coffee table while Tom took the garlic bread.

"I couldn't tell you." Tom shook his head.

"This smells fantastic." My stomach grumbled. Since I knew Tom was fixing dinner, I didn't eat anything from the café. "And I love Bette Davis, so you're not in any trouble this time."

"Are there any old movies you don't like?"

"I'm not big on Westerns. There are a few I like. John Wayne. Clint Eastwood. But without them, I'm not too interested. How about you?"

"*Citizen Kane.*"

"What? That movie is supposed to be the best movie of all time." I shoveled a huge forkful of spaghetti in my mouth. "I'm not shaying it ish, but that'sh what they shay." I held my hand up as I talked with my mouth full.

"I know. I've tried to watch it more than once and have fallen asleep every time. I don't think I've ever seen past the opening credits."

We were quiet for a few minutes as the movie started. Bette Davis emerged from her glorious Southern home and stood on the front terrace with a shotgun in her hands, ready to greet her relatives. She yelled at them in that beautiful Southern drawl. I loved it.

"This is really a rather gruesome movie," Tom said as we ate.

"For its day, yes." I took a sip of lemonade. "But how creative. How much fun it had to be for the actors to play these characters. They all have a touch of crazy in them. I'd love to walk around in long braids with garish makeup, screaming, *'Get out of here, Luke Standish! You smirkin' Judas!'* Don't tell me that doesn't sound like a blast. I might just start saying that around the café. What do you think?"

"I'd pay the price of admission." Tom chuckled.

As always, it was a wonderful time with Tom there. We finished every strand of spaghetti, the garlic bread, and a pint of chocolate-chocolate chip ice cream.

Treacle was in a ball, sleeping on the armchair the entire time. The fluffy kitty purred happily every time Tom reached to give him a scratch behind his ears or a stroke down his back.

"Well, it's getting late," Tom said after helping me load the dirty dishes into the dishwasher. "We both have to work tomorrow."

"Yeah, I guess so."

"Mind if I stop by the café on my way home tomorrow night?" He slipped his hand into mine as we walked to the front door.

"That would be nice."

"Can I sit in your section and get a cup of coffee?" He squeezed my hand.

"Sure."

"Can I make goo-goo eyes at you from across the café?"

"If you must." I chuckled.

"Can I draw little hearts with 'CG plus TW forever' on my napkin?"

"I won't stop you."

"Can I express my feelings for you in a poem accompanied by some interpretive dance?"

"I promised Aunt Astrid and Bea none of my suitors would do that anymore. You'll have to come up with something else."

For a few minutes at my front door, we kissed.

He got into his truck and waved goodbye as he pulled out of the driveway. I had forgotten all about Evelyn Elderflower.

Treacle must have felt very comfortable too. He stretched his paws out in front of him and yawned.

"Ready for bed, kitty?"

"*Yes.*" He hopped off the armchair and sauntered to the bedroom. I quickly put on my pajamas, washed my face, and brushed my teeth and was under the covers, feeling the heaviness of sleep falling over me, within minutes. It was a little after eleven.

I couldn't say what time it was when I became aware that something was wrong. My bedroom was still dark. In fact, I thought it was *unusually* dark, as if there might have been a power outage. You didn't realize how black darkness could be until all the outside lights you'd become used to were suddenly snuffed out.

That was my thought. A transformer had blown somewhere. The cold temps caused a wire to snap. Was the temperature in the house getting colder? The heat was electric, so it might be necessary to put on a few extra layers of clothes. But I could hear the hum of the furnace. There was no power outage.

So why was everything so dark? I tried to turn over to see the clock. At first, I thought that my body was just being lazy. My mind had woken up before my limbs had a chance to catch up. Sure. Why not? But as I tried to move, as I tried to turn my head to the right, I felt the panic start to spread. I couldn't move.

It was as though someone had put weights on my arms, legs, and chest. I could breathe. I could see. But I couldn't move. I was paralyzed. The blackness around me was so complete I had to squint to see if there was something holding me down. Had I gotten tied up? Had something fallen on my chest, holding me in place? But there was nothing there. Nothing that I could see. I tried to call out, but my voice was barely a whisper.

The adrenaline kicked in, making my heart pound wildly in my chest. Still, I couldn't move a muscle. My mouth felt as if it had been glued shut. Using every bit of strength I had, I pried my lips apart.

"Treacle." I felt my throat strain as I screamed in my head, but just a pitiful hiss came from my lips. Lying flat on my back, I felt completely exposed and vulnerable. What was happening? My breath came in panicked gasps. I was desperate to break these bonds, but nothing was working. In my mind, I could hear myself screaming for help. But only mumbles came out.

"*Cath!*" The voice wasn't mine. It wasn't Treacle. It was croaky and sinister, and I was terrified to admit that it was in my room and in my head at the same time.

As that thought entered my head, I saw the movement at the foot of my bed. I could only say that the thing began to unfold itself like a spider in the final stages of molting. First one arm appeared, stretching high up then bending at the elbow. The second arm slithered up and did the same. The hands were on the mattress. I felt them push against the springs as the thing pushed its torso up. A hunched body rolled up slowly, vertebra by vertebra until it towered over my bed. I still didn't see the head of the thing. I didn't want to. But my eyes were transfixed on it.

In my head, I was screaming. My lips twitched, but it felt as if my mouth were sewn shut. I could not utter a single word. Only pathetic whimpers came out. Even those, I couldn't be sure would have been audible to anyone. What if I was only hearing them in my head?

If only I could just move my arm. I struggled to make a fist. If I could muster enough strength to wiggle a pinky, I could break the spell. Terror sank its talons in my heart as I stared at the thing at the end of my bed as the head finally rolled up.

It was slow and deliberate, as a cobra might raise its head as it prepared to attack. The thing kept getting bigger and bigger until I was sure it had filled my entire room. Still, I tried to pull myself out of the bed. Even to fall on the floor would be better than facing this black shadowy thing. As I stared, still screaming in my head with no sound coming out of my mouth, it opened its eyes. They were red slits that glared back at me. These were the eyes of the rat that Treacle had seen in the corner. It wasn't a rat at all.

Before I could blink back the tears of terror that were pooling in my eyes, I saw something else. The teeth. That blackness, the most hopeless and deep blackness I'd ever seen, peeled back to reveal jagged teeth behind an evil grin. This monster began to lean closer. First the left arm crawled over my legs, then the right followed. I felt its weight pushing the entire mattress into the floor.

If it got to my face, I would die. I just knew it. Something inside said I'd die of fright and it would steal my soul. It would eat it or shred it or something equally horrifying. If only I could move. If only I was strong enough to scream.

The head wagged back and forth as it hissed and growled. Inside my head, I could hear thousands of screaming voices that were saying something to me. I couldn't make out the words, but the tone of the voices was unmistakable. They hated me.

*"You!"*

That voice, I recognized.

*"I'm not through with you!"*

It was Treacle. Suddenly, he was on my chest, facing the shadow person and hissing madly. He was furious. His fur stood out. His mouth was pulled back to reveal his sharp teeth, and thankfully, I could feel his claws through the blanket. I was never so happy to feel those sharp needles as I was then.

The shadow recoiled and swatted at Treacle, who returned the blow in kind. It was as if I were watching a film run backward on a reel. The shadow person screamed in all its hideous voices and slithered back to the edge of the bed. Before it folded itself back up, it pointed and glared at me.

Treacle lunged at the thing, swiping his sharp claws, but before he could snag it, the thing disappeared. At that same second, I sat bolt upright in bed.

"Cath! My gosh! What on earth happened? Quick. Come inside."

My aunt tugged her robe closed against the chill in the air. I barely had my snow boots on and a thin throw blanket around my shoulders with Treacle in my arms.

"Can I stay with you tonight?" I sniffled.

"Of course you can." She shut and locked the door behind me and led me into the kitchen.

"I'm sorry I woke you up," I said as I set Treacle down on the floor. Within seconds, Marshmallow was in the living room, asking what had happened while giving Treacle a loving nudge with her head.

"I was actually awake. Now, tell me what happened."

I looked at the clock and nearly choked. It was

barely after midnight. I was sure that it was at least three in the morning. It felt as if I had been trapped on that bed for hours. But Tom had just left a little over an hour prior.

Over a steaming-hot cup of tea, I told my aunt what had just gone on at my house. The more I told her, the more serious her expression became. It was the first time I was more afraid of my aunt's response than what I had told her about.

"So? What do you think?"

I knew what it meant when my aunt didn't answer right away. It meant she was waiting for the anger to subside. She'd had the same reaction a couple times when I was in high school. One particular time that came to mind was when I had almost been suspended for three days for finally standing up to Darla Castellan. It was senior year and about time I did something.

Darla was running off at the mouth about my best bud, Min Parks. He was a gentle, peaceful guy and the perfect target for a bully. I'd heard Darla making fun of him and told her I'd make sure she didn't make it to graduation if she didn't stop talking about him.

In all honesty, my plot had been to break my aunt's rule just once and use my magic to give Darla an award-winning case of boils or maybe have her develop a twenty-four-hour goiter. It would be enough to keep her out of graduation—give her a big dose of humility.

My aunt knew that was all I was capable of. Bea knew it.

But when Darla had the nerve to report me to Vice Principal Lewis, I was fit to be tied. For four years, that bimbo had used me to sharpen her claws, and then she had the nerve to tell on me?

I sat in Lewis's office and waited for my aunt to arrive. When she finally showed up, I wasn't sure who was more scared. Me or him.

"You understand we have to take every threat seriously, Mrs. Greenstone."

My aunt sat there and stared at Lewis for a long while. He squirmed in his seat as she studied him.

"It's just so out of character for Cath to lash out. We know she and Miss Castellan have had clashes in the past. We felt this time it was necessary to call you." It was a real treat to watch him stutter.

"So what do you think we should do about the situation, Mrs. Greenstone?"

Aunt Astrid was not looking at the dimensions around Vice Principal Lewis. She was staring right at him. Her face was not the gentle, soft face I was used to seeing every day. It was fixed and focused, as if she was taking aim. After a solid minute of staring right at him, my aunt finally gave Lewis an answer.

"Mr. Lewis, my niece has been going to school here for four years. How many times have I been in your office?"

"I believe this is the first time."

"Mr. Lewis, she's never been in your office in four years, but two weeks before graduation, you call me in to tell me she might be suspended for threatening a classmate. The classmate that has been harassing her for four years."

"I-I had no idea that was taking place," he stuttered.

"You just told me you knew the girls had clashes in the past. Are you lying?"

"Well, I meant to say that…"

My aunt sat there stoically while Mr. Lewis blathered on about what he meant and what he said, and before the meeting was over, he was telling my aunt there would be no repercussions and this would be chalked up as a learning experience for everyone involved.

She had won that battle for me. It looked as if she was ready for another round, except this one, the bully wasn't just the popular girl in high school. She called this bully the Gazzo.

"You look exhausted." My aunt put her hand gently underneath my chin. "Like you've been up for days. Go on into my room and get some sleep."

Aunt Astrid had the biggest bedroom in the house. Her four-poster bed was piled high with downy mattress covers and a down comforter that would make the most delicate Southern belle swoon with envy.

"Will you be coming in there soon?"

"I should sleep in the bed with you?" she asked as if she were my own mother.

I nodded.

"Well, I've got a few things to do first. How about Marshmallow and Treacle join you for starters."

Both cats heard the call and slunk bravely up to wrap lovingly around my ankles.

"*Come on, Cath. We'll take first watch,*" Treacle said.

"Okay. Thanks, Aunt Astrid," I mumbled.

It wasn't until I woke up the next morning that I realized my aunt had never come to bed. Treacle and Marshmallow were curled up on the bed, one at my head and the other at my feet. I also found an extra body lying along my side. Bea's cat, Peanut Butter, had joined the watch.

I could smell coffee and heard quiet voices talking. They were not like the voices I heard screaming at me in my head. They were gentle, loving, and familiar.

As I shuffled down the stairs and to the kitchen, I saw Bea and her mom sitting in front of a roaring fire with several of Aunt Astrid's books on witchcraft spread out in front of them.

Before I could say anything, the cats bounded down the stairs first.

"You're up. You poor thing." Bea jumped up and ran to hug me. "What an ordeal. Let me fix you some tea." She turned and went to the kitchen.

"Did you get any sleep?" I asked my aunt.

"I was busy doing research."

"On the shadowy figure in my bedroom." I shuddered before grabbing a patchwork quilt to throw around my shoulders.

"That and our friends the Elderflowers." Aunt Astrid winked.

"What did you find out about them? And how?"

"Mom pulled an all-nighter and went hard-core digging on those people. Hard-core," Bea said over the running tap. "She hasn't told me anything. Said we need to wait until tonight."

"Tonight? How come?" I pouted. "The sooner I

know what that thing was, the sooner we can get our mojos together and knock the thing back to the eighth dimension where it belongs."

"Tonight, girls. I promise. Right now, we need to get ready for work. And you are not going back into your house until I've done a thorough smudging of the place. You're obviously long overdue."

A smudging was the practice of cleaning all the negativity and bad boogies out of a house. My aunt was particularly good at them. She had a way of waving the sage bundle that made the ringlets of smoke look like links of a chain before they dissipated.

## 14

### AUGURY

By the time Bea flipped the Open sign to Closed, we were ready to burst. Aunt Astrid had kept us in the dark all day long. She would not address the monster that attacked last night or talk about Evelyn. It was infuriating.

"Okay, girls. Bea, grab that leftover spinach salad. Cath, there is a bag of honey crisp apples in the kitchen. Go get them, and both of you come to the bunker."

Within seconds, we were down in the cozy hideaway.

"Do you need these things for a spell?" I asked as I set the bag of apples on a small side table next to the love seat.

"No. I didn't eat today, and I'm hungry. You both

need to eat something too. We are going to need to keep our strength up for this one."

Reluctantly, I took a heaping paper plate full of spinach salad from Bea, who handed it over with the most defiant look on her face. Vegetables and me weren't the best of friends. Aunt Astrid handed me a giant apple, and I doled out the bottled water.

"Last night after you arrived, Cath, I had an augury."

Bea and I both held our breath.

"An augury?" Bea immediately began to panic. "Like when we were kids?"

We hadn't heard the word *augury* for over a decade. It was in reference to an incident that happened when Bea and I were still in high school. We had come home laughing and gossiping, as sixteen-year-old girls were prone to do. When we walked into the house, we both felt the shift in the air. Something was wrong. Bea and I didn't live in the house that Aunt Astrid lived in now. She and my uncle Eagle Eye lived in a cute farmhouse on the other side of town. It creaked and groaned and held all the nooks and crannies farmhouses had, like a fruit cellar, a tornado shelter, and a pantry off the kitchen. There were decorative wrought-iron grates over the heating vents and two ceiling fans on the front porch.

"Mom?" Bea called, but we got no answer.

*"Marshmallow?"* I called telepathically. *"Marshmallow? Are you here?"*

We split up and darted through the house. It was Bea's scream that made me run from the pantry up the flight of stairs to Aunt Astrid's bedroom.

My aunt was sobbing in the corner of the room.

"What are you doing home?" she cried.

"Mom. We're out of school. Of course we're home," Bea said. "What's the matter? What happened?"

Aunt Astrid just shook her head. She wouldn't say anything as she pushed herself to her feet. Bea went to hug her, and that was when it happened.

"Don't touch me!" Aunt Astrid screamed, making us both jump back. "Don't you dare touch me!"

She stormed out of the room, hysterical, and locked herself in the bathroom.

We were terrified. But what could we do?

"Where is Marshmallow?" I put my hand on Bea's shoulder to steady her. "Maybe she knows what happened."

This time, Bea and I stayed together. We held hands

like two little girls as we searched in all the rooms, starting with the basement. Like all cats, Marshmallow liked it in the dark, where she prowled for mice and spiders and the occasional snake that would work its way into the house. But she wasn't there.

We searched the main floor, even checking in the china cabinet and hall coat closet. Nothing. Finally, back upstairs, we heard the heart-wrenching sound of Aunt Astrid trying to control her crying. But in addition to that, there was an answer.

I was screaming the cat's name in my head while Bea called out for her. Finally, I heard a faint reply.

*"Here! I'm here!"* It was coming from high up.

"The attic? What in the world is she doing up there?"

The attic was a place Bea and I would occasionally spend time, especially in the winter when the hot air from the furnace would rise and make it toasty warm.

Instead of having a trap door in the ceiling and a ladder that would cascade down, we got to the attic by a short flight of steep steps that were hidden in a hall closet.

My aunt kept empty mason jars and a couple boxes of Christmas decorations and normal things stacked on the steps.

Bea and I bolted over them like Olympic runners. Marshmallow was at the small square window when we finally reached her. She jumped into my arms, clawing and trembling terribly.

"What happened to Mom?" Bea sobbed.

Marshmallow pushed her head against my chin.

*"Marshmallow? What happened to Aunt Astrid?"* I asked her.

*"We were sitting in the kitchen. You know how she had been trying to map some of the portals she saw."*

My aunt had extensive notes on some of the dimensions she had been able to see. Some of them, she even visited briefly in a remote viewing capacity. For her own knowledge and for posterity, she was diagramming them. Some people scrapbooked. My aunt drew blueprints to other dimensions.

*"Well, something surprised her."*

I repeated this to Bea.

"What happened?"

*"It just sprang on her. Whatever it was forced visions into her head. She tried not to see them, but it wasn't her eyes. It used her gift against her. She tried to get away. When I tried to touch her and help her fight, she tossed me in the attic and slammed the door shut."*

I was crying as I quietly repeated these words to Bea.

"That's why she didn't want me to touch her." This was the only time Bea ever regretted having the gift of being an empath. She just wanted to hug her mother. She just wanted to be a girl comforting her mother. That seemed like such a simple request, yet Bea couldn't touch her without feeling what her mother had.

We went downstairs.

Quickly, Bea brewed a special tea with chamomile, lavender, and neathrill, a magical herb that helped when witches experienced extreme burnout.

"It can't hurt, right?" Bea asked as she poured the tea into her mom's favorite teacup and added a slice of lemon. Just the way Aunt Astrid liked it.

We went upstairs and knocked on the bathroom door.

My aunt mumbled a thank you and asked us to leave the tea outside the door. She assured us she'd be okay and would be downstairs shortly. We were to get our homework done.

We sat at the kitchen table and did our work as the sun began to set.

Finally, Aunt Astrid appeared in a clean dress, her hair wet from a shower.

Her eyes were puffy from crying, as were ours.

"Bea." She finally spoke. "I didn't mean to yell at you, honey."

Bea jumped up from her chair to run to her mother, but Aunt Astrid stopped her with her hand in front of her while taking a step back.

"No. You can't touch me," she instructed us. "If you do, I'm afraid you'll feel what was there."

"What was it, Mom? What did this to you?"

"None of us are experts at this, honey. I want you to remember that. We have these talents on loan from the Great Creator. And sometimes we get abused because of it. That doesn't mean we shouldn't use them. It means we have to be more careful."

Marshmallow had sidled up to me. I stroked her head.

"I had a vision, is all. No. It wasn't so much a vision as it was an augury," Aunt Astrid said as fresh tears filled her eyes. "I didn't want it. I didn't invite it. But it came to me, and now I have to figure out what to do with it."

"What was it?" I asked.

My aunt shook her head. She never told us. Whatever it was, she kept it to herself. If she ever had a vision like this again, she never told us that either. But she took some serious steps to protect herself from this kind of attack.

We knew Aunt Astrid was as tough as nails. But what she had experienced back then wasn't really a vision. She had visions and premonitions and could get glimpses of the future and past just sitting at the back table with a customer and reading their tea leaves.

I'd call what happened all those years ago an assault. But that's just me. I had a paranormal parasite sucking the life out of me once. The world of witchcraft could be just as painful as this one could be.

Now, Bea and I were feeling like those confused teenagers again. After my attack, it was only logical to think something came after Aunt Astrid too.

"No, girls. Not like that." She shook her head sadly and looked at me. "What I saw was something that could be used to our benefit. But it will require that we all agree to do it. If one has the slightest hesitation, we'll need to find another way."

"Aunt Astrid, I don't mean to be rude, but could you just get to the point?" I was nervously shredding a red paper napkin I had grabbed from upstairs.

"Yes. Be patient with me. I have to go forward to

go back. The Elderflowers are listed in *The Catalog of Harbingers*."

*The Catalog of Harbingers* was what I'd imagine the royal family's list of relatives for the past several centuries would look like. You'd have your Elizabeths and your Dianas, and you'd also have the lesser-known Hortenses and Thomasinas. You'd know whom they married, how many children they had, and whom those children married. You'd also find what they did for a living, what their level of witchcraft was, as well as every scandal there might have been carefully documented. Apparently, the Elderflowers had a slightly bent family tree.

"They are not witches. Due to an incestuous relationship back in the 1800s, the bloodline was skewed. Had things gone "normally," we might have found ourselves with kindred spirits living just on the other end of town. But according to the catalog, their comingling sort of stunted the natural growth of sorcery." She cleared her throat. "That's as graphic as I care to get. Now, to go back to the beginning."

My aunt sat down in the straight-backed chair that I had snagged from a thrift store for five dollars. "Cath, after you told me what happened, I went to find a description of the creature you described."

I shivered.

"But before I even got past three pages, my vision started to blur. I thought it was typical eyestrain. Not uncommon for a woman my age, especially when I like candlelight more than reading lamps." She chuckled. "I went to the bathroom to splash a little cold water on my face, and that was when I saw it in the mirror."

"A shadow person?" I gasped.

"No. Evelyn."

"What?" Bea's mouth hung open.

Aunt Astrid nodded.

"Did she talk to you?" I asked.

"I don't think the girl even knew she had shown up in my mirror. I think she was asleep. Just like we've been fretting over her these past couple of days, she has been doing the same with us. Whether it is some of that old Elderflower psychic energy forcing its way to the surface or just blind luck, she got a message across."

"What was the message?"

"She's trapped," Aunt Astrid replied sadly.

"Trapped? I don't understand." I looked at Bea, who shrugged.

"I'm not sure what it all means either. But that little girl needs our help." Aunt Astrid took a sip of water and cleared her throat.

"I don't mean to sound selfish or anything, but any idea what that might have to do with the thing that came in my house? We still haven't figured out what that was. Or have you, and you're just not telling me? Because it was scary. I mean super-scary. Like *scary*."

"Was it scary?" Bea teased.

"Poop-your-pants scary," I replied.

"I found a shady character who not only fit your description but also was in line with our Gazzo theory." Aunt Astrid sipped her water again. "We've got a spectral shylock, and he's going to step in front of anyone who might get in the way of his getting paid in full."

"He was at the Elderflower house. That was who I saw in the window." I explained the shadowy figure looking at me just before I took off running.

"He saw your face, Cath. He's going to be looking for you," Aunt Astrid said sternly. "That means he'll be looking for all of us. And bullies like him—if he thinks he can't do the job himself, he'll get backup. Fighting dirty isn't a problem for our Gazzo."

"But that doesn't explain how the Gazzo got called." Bea shoveled a forkful of spinach in her mouth.

"It wasn't Evelyn," I stated. "I'm sure of that."

"Cath is right," Aunt Astrid said. "It's time we start looking at the other Elderflowers, starting with the sisters. I have a plan. But this has to be timed perfectly. I don't want to tip them off. If that happens, we'll all be getting a visit from the shadow people."

I was up for anything if it meant never seeing that Gazzo-shadow person again. Too bad it didn't work out as we had planned.

## ❧ 15 ❧

## CIRCLED IN BLACK

"I just need you to fake a limp or something," I muttered to Treacle as I pulled him from my car. "We aren't looking to get you checked in overnight. Just a simple exam."

*"Are you sure? Because I can fake a malady. You just say the word. I can do stomach cramps. I can do fainting. I can also vomit on command if you thought it might be helpful,"* Treacle answered enthusiastically.

"No, Sir Lawrence Olivier. Geez, since when did you catch the acting bug? Just limp. This isn't for an Oscar. It's just to give me a chance to talk to the woman."

Treacle and I were about to walk into Gail Elderflower's veterinary clinic. She had been in business in Wonder Falls for a little over two years, according to what I'd researched. The same went for Fern and her dermatology office. Together, they had a little over four years in business.

"This is a lot fancier than your vet," I said as I carried Treacle into the office. It was set up like a human doctor's office. Except instead of regular health and financial magazines, we had our pick of *Dog Fancy, Cat Universe, Critters,* and *Healthy Pets.* There was a carpet-covered cat tower to the left of the waiting room. On the right side was a patch of green Astroturf. I assumed that was for the nervous canines that were too riled up to go outside.

The receptionist was wearing purple nursing scrubs and at least a pound of makeup.

"Good afternoon," she said. "Can I help you?"

"Yeah, this is Treacle Greenstone. I'm Cath Greenstone. I called earlier for the doctor to look at my cat's paw. He just started limping."

"Fine." The receptionist handed me a stack of papers attached to a clipboard without smiling. I took a seat and began to fill them out.

The waiting room was like a zoo. There were five dogs: a couple of mutts, one with a white circle around his right eye, and the other black with a gray muzzle; one very pampered Pekinese, which barked and yipped every few seconds; an American bulldog that was the equivalent of Arnold

Schwarzenegger in the canine muscle group, sitting proudly and obediently next to his equally proud owner; and a feisty dachshund that tugged at his leash. He didn't seem to have anyone he wanted to talk to in particular, but he wanted to be free from his leash.

There was one woman with a cat in a travel box. The cat seemed more annoyed than anything, although the few meows that came from the crate were pitiful sounding.

"It's okay, baby," the owner said soothingly. "It's just your checkup."

Treacle sat calmly in my lap.

Over the doors to the examining rooms were some strange symbols carved into wood. At first glance, I thought they read dogs and cats in Latin or Spanish or Chinese. But then I realized they were not a language but symbols.

Quickly, I reached in my purse and pulled out a blank check. I started to scribble the designs on it. I finished the paperwork about Treacle's health history and handed it back to the receptionist. Now Treacle and I waited.

That was when I noticed one person was sitting in the corner at the farthest end of the waiting room with a white rat perched on his shoulder. He was lanky, had a gray beard, and wore a flannel button-down shirt with gray trousers and a pea coat.

The rat looked like a statue at first glance. Then it moved.

*"Is that guy really here?"* I asked Treacle.

*"He is, and he isn't. This is no ordinary vet office. Something else is here."*

*"Is it ten feet tall with red eyes and a couple rows of jagged teeth?"*

*"Thank goodness, no. But it isn't happy we're here."*

*"How come?"* I asked.

*"I don't know. But I get the feeling we're going to find out."*

As with any doctor's office, we were prepared to wait. I spoke with some of the pets. The said they hated coming here. The mutts were the most articulate.

*"She's mean,"* the gray-muzzled pooch said. *"She doesn't like animals."*

*"How can that be?"* I asked. *"Do you misbehave?"*

*"No,"* they replied together. *"We behave. She still doesn't like us."*

I knew not to take the dogs too seriously. They were such honest and dedicated animals that they might think Gail didn't like them because she didn't shower them with treats and kisses.

It was about forty-five minutes before Gail Elder-flower stepped through the door and called Treacle by name. I waved and scooped Treacle back into my arms. He'd snuggled down on the seat next to me while I maneuvered the clipboard.

"What seems to be the trouble?" Gail asked pleasantly enough.

I gave her a quick description then began the plan Aunt Astrid had outlined for us.

"You are Marie Elderflower's daughter. I wasn't sure when I saw the name in the phone book, so I thought I'd take a chance."

"That's me. Don't you have a regular vet?" she asked while looking over Treacle, who had become frozen like a statue.

"I do, but he's on sabbatical. I didn't like the replacement he had."

"Of course," she muttered. "Can I see him walk?"

I nodded, picked Treacle up, and set him on the floor. It was almost comical to see him hobble around. He was really hamming it up. But when Gail leaned down to pick him up, he swiped at her and hissed.

"How's your sister doing?" I asked while she watched Treacle.

"She's fine. Why wouldn't she be?"

"Well, you know how teenagers are. They can be demanding, especially after losing a parent."

"Oh, you mean Evelyn." She practically spat the words. Then she looked at me as if she suddenly realized I owed her money for a bet I'd lost. "How do you know about that?"

"I'm sorry, Gail. I thought you remembered me. My name is Cath Greenstone. I was at the funeral for your mom. Your sister seemed, well, distant."

It was as if a switch went off behind her eyes. Suddenly, Gail's face didn't relay bored repetition but hostility.

"Did she. I blame my mother for that. She spoiled the girl to no end. Wait a second. You were the woman at the coffee shop. The one feeding Evelyn stories."

"What?" I might have been on an intelligence mission, but nowhere did it say I was supposed to get my behind handed to me. "Feeding her stories? I haven't seen Evelyn since the funeral."

Instinct told me to get Treacle. I reached down and scooped him into my arms.

"That's a lie." Gail glared at me and at Treacle. "I don't know what kind of game you are playing with that brat, but you better take your cat and get out of here."

"What about his paw?" I meekly asked.

"I don't know, and I don't care. Good day, Miss Greenstone. Don't come back."

Without another word, Gail left the office, mumbled something to the receptionist, and then disappeared down another corridor.

Without hesitation, Treacle leaped from my arms and trotted down the hallway.

"Treacle!" I shouted but made very little attempt to catch him. "Wait, kitty! Where are you going?"

"Great!" the receptionist snapped. "You need to keep control of your animal. He should be in a crate."

"He doesn't like crates," I muttered. It was true. Treacle didn't like crates. But he'd get in one if he absolutely had to. I wasn't going to tell the receptionist that.

She jumped up from her chair to chase the big black cat as he darted after Gail. In the meantime, the entire lobby erupted into chaos. Dogs were barking and pulling on their leashes. Cats were swiping their hands out of cages and crates to snag anything that might come near them.

I pretended to be distraught and leaned on the receptionist's desk. While she was occupied, I looked over things. The appointment book was full of patients to be coming in.

"Treacle!" I shouted. "Come back!"

I flipped through the desk drawers and found nothing of value. When I turned and headed down the hallway, I saw the receptionist with her back to me as Treacle was safely underneath a shelf with heavy bags of dog food stacked on it.

*"I'm good, Cath! Keep looking! This is fun!"*

*"Don't get yourself hurt. Just give me two minutes!"* I replied.

Just then, Gail came bursting out of a small office.

"What is going on?" she yelled.

"I'm so sorry. Treacle just bolted out of my arms!" I whined. "He's hiding under that shelf! Oh, the poor thing!" I grabbed Gail's arm. "Please don't let him get hurt. What are we going to do? He won't come out!"

Gail grimaced and clenched her teeth, pushing past me to get to the receptionist. That poor girl was on her knees, peeking underneath the shelf as Treacle hissed and swatted as if he were afflicted with rabies.

I quickly ducked into Gail's office and looked around. There were strange symbols over her door too. I walked up to her desk and noticed a flat calendar spread out with just a few papers across it.

Funny that the day of her mother's funeral was circled in black but nothing was written in it. Prior to that, the day Marie died was also circled, but nothing was written indicating why.

As I skimmed the remaining days of the month, I saw nothing but one mark. Three days from today, another date was circled in black. Nothing was written in the square.

"What are you doing?" Gail screamed. "Get out of my office!"

"I-I'm so s-sorry," I stuttered. "I was feeling faint. I thought I was going to pass out, so I came to your desk to steady myself. Can I get a glass of water?"

I knew I was pushing it. So did Gail.

"You go and get your cat and get out of my office." She pointed a trembling hand at the door.

Throwing my arm dramatically over my eyes, I staggered to the door. What was the worst she could do? As soon as that thought came to mind, I saw something swipe at me from the corner of my eye. When I looked, there was nothing there. Nothing that I could see. But I felt it.

"Here, kitty, kitty!" I yelled. Within seconds, Treacle was at my side, and we quickly made our way toward the red exit sign. That was when the rat man appeared. He stood in front of the door. The rat was still on his shoulder.

"Excuse me," I barked loudly over the rest of the barking that was going on. Treacle trotted two paces ahead of me. I watched the rat man jump out of my cat's way and back up against the doorjamb. But as I passed him, I heard that same raspy voice I'd heard the other night.

"*Cath!*" It shouted inside my head.

When I looked back at him over my shoulder, there was nothing there but a dark shadow. I didn't waste time. Treacle read my mind, and we ran out of the vet's office and toward the car.

"That could have gone better." I panted as we jumped in and drove out of the parking lot before my door was even all the way shut.

"*Did you see it?*" Treacle asked.

"See what? The look on Gail's face when she realized we were bamboozling her? Yes. She's pretty mad."

"*No. Did you see the shadows?*"

My hands instantly began to sweat as I gripped the steering wheel. I swallowed hard even though my mouth had gone dry.

"The one by the door? Yes. I saw him."

*"No. The other one."*

"What other one?"

*"I thought you looked right at it. It dove at you but then disappeared."*

"I saw something move out of the corner of my eye. In fact, I've been seeing that a lot. Something moving out of the corner of my eye, but when I turn to see, there is nothing there. What is that?"

*"I think it's the shadow people."*

"Shadow *people*? You mean you think there are more than one?"

*"Yes. I think there is a gang of them."*

"Do you think they are just around us, or do you think they are at the doctor's office too?"

*"I think wherever there is an Elderflower, there are shadow people."*

We hurried to get home to my aunt's house. I wasn't allowed back in my place until Aunt Astrid took care of business, so we let ourselves in and went immediately to the fridge.

"I wonder if there is anything in any of Aunt Astrid's books that look like these weird symbols. Did you see them all over the vet's office? They were over the doors."

Treacle nuzzled up to Marshmallow, who came to say hello.

I went into my aunt's study and began skimming the books on her shelves. It was amazing how many tomes she had collected over the years that answered so many questions. If we didn't guard our witchcraft so tightly, this collection of books would probably fetch a small fortune.

"Let's see. Spells. Incantations. Vision interpretation. Demons. Haunted locations. I'm glad she has these organized by subject, or else we could be here all day." I strained to see some of the higher shelves. My aunt's study was a cozy place, but I had seen some chocolate pie in the fridge, so nothing was going to keep me in the study for very long.

"Aha! There you are, you sneaky devil. *Denotations of the Netherworld, Volume One and Two.* Yikes. This ought to have something in it, right?"

I stood on a chair to get the giant tome off the shelf. It was dusty and had that wonderful old-book smell that was romantic and thrilling all at once.

"This reminds me of studying for school. I swear my algebra book was this big," I grumbled.

*"It wasn't that big. You thought it was because you hate math,"* Treacle said.

"Your point being?" I rolled my eyes. "Hey, what would you call that rat man standing by the door?

Was he a shape-shifter? A shadow person? A harbinger of doom and gloom?"

"Rat man?" Marshmallow asked.

Treacle gave Marshmallow a blow-by-blow description of what happened at the vet's office.

"Treacle, did you hear that man call my name?"

My cat looked at me and purred.

"*Nope.*"

"I swear, it sounded like the same voice, the same growl as that thing that was in the bedroom the other night. But this guy was solid form, right? And he had a rat on his shoulder, right?"

"*That wasn't a man.*"

"*How do you know?*" Marshmallow read my mind.

"*Because what Cath saw was mostly man, and what I saw was mostly shadow. He was the goon at the gate. He was there to make sure that nothing happened to Gail that would cause problems.*"

"So was he her bodyguard?"

"*Bodyguard or prison guard. It's hard to tell.*"

I hoisted the book of symbols up on my shoulder and walked back to the kitchen. After dropping it on the counter, I pulled the pie out of the fridge and cut myself a wedge.

"So you think he was there to keep an eye on Gail

for one reason or another?" I asked around a mouthful of pie.

*"That's what I think, and I don't think he was alone."*

"Well, let's see what we can find in this book." I sighed at its size. "The beginning of every book starts on page one."

I grabbed the doodles from my purse and held them in one hand while I flipped the pages with the other. In between, I devoured two slices of chocolate pie and two glasses of milk.

It was nearly three o'clock when Bea and Aunt Astrid finally arrived back home. Their story was even more treacherous than mine.

## 16

## SPECTERS

"What took you so long?" I asked as they came through the front door. "I was worried sick about you two. Haven't you ever heard of a telephone? That's it. You are both grounded."

"Very funny," Bea said as she helped her mother in the house.

"Aunt Astrid? Are you all right?" I quickly stopped the teasing and rushed to help. My aunt was pale, but she still had that wild twinkle in her eyes.

"I'll be fine. We had to get out of that office a lot faster than when we walked in. So, what happened at the vet's office?"

Hearing my aunt's voice, Marshmallow jumped off the couch, where she'd been snuggling with Treacle. She hopped up on the table behind the sofa and waited, demanding an explanation.

*"I told her to take it easy, but she never listens to me,"* Marshmallow said.

*"That's because I'm the only one who can hear you. Be patient, and let's hear what happened,"* I replied, stroking the cat's head.

"I know, Marshmallow. I'm late," Aunt Astrid said as she lifted the cat in her arms like a baby and slung her over her shoulder. Marshmallow purred happily. "I've got to sit down."

"I'll get you some water, Mom."

"Tea would be better," my aunt said. "And a slice of chocolate pie if Cath hasn't eaten the whole thing." She winked at me.

"I only had two slices," I said as I stepped over to the kitchen to help Bea. As the kettle began to bubble, I told them what had happened at the vet office.

"So, it was quite a spectacle," I finished. "But we did get rough sketches of the designs over the doors. Maybe you'll recognize them from something you've seen before." I handed my drawings to my aunt.

"Oh, I do recognize these. They were at the doctor's office too."

"What do they mean?" I went back into the kitchen to get teacups for Bea, my aunt, and myself.

"They are blinders," my aunt answered with a sad click of her tongue. I didn't ask any more questions. I waited for the tea, brought my aunt a slice of pie, and took a seat next to Treacle, who was casually waving his tail over the side of the ottoman he had chosen to lie on. I wanted to hear what happened.

"Normally, I'd suspect the Elderflowers were into something that they'd lost control of. But that isn't really the case. Not based on what we saw."

Aunt Astrid and Bea were just planning on scoping out Fern's dermatology practice. But there was a sign on the door that invited walk-ins for a free consultation.

"We'd be stupid not to take advantage of that," my aunt said. "So I drummed up a quick skin ailment on my shoulder, and Bea and I walked in."

"What kind of skin ailment?" I asked curiously.

"What does it matter?" Bea asked around a mouthful of chocolate pie.

"Just curious. Did you make it gross and oozy so she'd have to keep you there a long time?"

"No, Cath. I just made it a cross between ring-worm and prickly heat."

"Eww." I wrinkled my nose.

"It wasn't really anything. Just a mirage. But I couldn't walk in without anything to show her."

"You should have given Bea a wart on her nose."

"Funny, cuz. Very funny." Bea brought the TV tray with three cups of tea on it and set it on the coffee table before taking a seat next to her mother. I chuckled because Bea was one of those lucky ladies blessed with perfectly smooth skin, bright, wide eyes, and naturally long eyelashes. A wart on her nose would have been as hokey and out of place as a wad of chewed-up gum on the Mona Lisa.

"So, with my fake lesion, we walked in and told the nurse at the front desk we'd just walked in and were hoping the doctor could make a suggestion as to what to do. But even that turned out to be more troubling than we expected."

My aunt went on to describe a spiderwebby haze that hung over the place.

"Fern Elderflower obviously had a cloaking spell of some kind over the place. It was a phantasm that had settled over the entire office."

"But you couldn't see it?" I asked Bea.

"I saw a state-of-the-art office with spotless walls and windows and floors. Everything was neat and orderly. Everyone was professional, if not frigidly so. But had I not been on a data-collecting mission, I wouldn't have noticed anything strange. You know how some women professionals are. They feel they have to be tougher or more serious than the men in their profession." Bea rolled her eyes. "I just assumed Fern Elderflower was one of those kinds of women."

"The lobby was filled with people," Aunt Astrid added. "She's obviously developed a reputation, but not everything was as it seemed. Some of those patients, I could see right through."

"What do you mean?" I asked.

"Exactly what I said. They were not real people. They were specters. Phantoms."

"To me, everyone looked relatively normal, except the nurse at the front counter. She looked very intense, like she had just found out someone keyed the side of her car," Bea said. "So, when I told her that my mother had a weird something on her shoulder, she quickly handed me a clipboard full of paper and a pen and went back to her work behind the desk. Normally, a doctor's office asks about insurance first. Not a peep from this one."

"Now that in itself is suspect." I shook my head and folded my arms over my chest. "Don't trust an outfit that doesn't ask about insurance when insurance is who pays them. Totally suspicious."

They said they took their stack of paperwork and halfheartedly filled it out while looking around the office.

"That was when I noticed the symbols over the doors." Aunt Astrid took a huge forkful of pie and washed it down with a sip of tea. "Now, I could be wrong, but I think those were what was keeping the haze over the entire place."

My aunt went on to say that having one of those symbols meant nothing. But using them together was like plugging a few cords of Christmas lights into one another. They worked together and stretched the electricity, or in this case, the paranormal illusion, over the whole building.

"But that sounds like witchcraft, and you said the Elderflowers aren't witches," I replied.

"They aren't. They are borrowing from someone," Bea said.

"Or some*thing*," my aunt added.

After completing the paperwork and handing everything back to the nurse, they sat in the waiting room for an hour. Finally, their name was called, and they were led to a smaller room, where they waited for another twenty minutes. That was when Aunt Astrid saw it.

"We aren't alone," Aunt Astrid had said to Bea. "Over there in the corner. Do you see that shadow?"

Bea squinted.

"That was one thing I noticed," Bea said to me. "I kept seeing things moving out of the corner of my eye like a person falling or someone lunging toward us. But every time I looked in the direction of the movement, there was nothing there."

"That has been happening to me too," I admitted.

"There was something there, all right," Aunt Astrid said. "And now we had one in the room with us."

She described it as a faint, pulsing discoloration against the wall. Had she not had the ability to see through to other dimensions, she would have completely missed it, as Bea had. But her keen sense of her surroundings made the phantom's attempt at camouflage unsuccessful.

"Before I could attempt to connect with it, Fern walked in," Aunt Astrid said before eating her final bite of pie.

"Connect with it? Why in the world would you try to do that?" I asked while debating whether or not I should have one more slice of pie myself.

"We have to know what we are dealing with. There is a reason these things are around the Elderflowers. But like I said, before I could reach out to it, she walked in. She wasn't alone either."

My aunt went on to describe Fern entering the small examination room while being followed by two hulking shadow people.

"They weren't as defined as what you saw, Cath. But they were there, and they were not about to let Bea or me find out anything about Fern."

"How do you know that?" I asked nervously.

"I could see them talking to her. Like a criminal in front of an investigation panel, Fern Elderflower wasn't going to say or do anything they didn't approve of. The scary thing was that she didn't seem to mind their influence."

"I couldn't see them as clearly as Mom, but by this time, I felt them," Bea continued the story.

"So, Mrs. Greenstone. You are here for a free consultation about a mark on your shoulder. Did you complete your paperwork?" Fern asked coldly. "We cannot do a consultation without first having all your personal information."

"Of course." Bea smiled but got nothing in return.

"So, tell me about your history. Have you ever had anything like this before? Do you smoke?

Consume alcohol? Is there a history of skin cancer or any other similar afflictions in your family?"

I wondered if Aunt Astrid mentioned our deceased great-aunt Isobol, who had a revenge spell backfire. After finding her lover two-timing her, she decided the female who was sharing his affection should be taught a lesson. So, with eye of newt and wing of bat and wart of a horny toad, she was determined to give this woman a horribly disfiguring skin condition that would render her unlovable by any man. But as with most revenge spells, combined with mediocre witchcraft and a maximum level of hypocrisy, Great-Aunt Isobol ended up not giving the mistress a crippling affliction. Instead, she gave herself a severe case of acne that would flare up whenever she was out in public. The pustules would be known to violently erupt at times. It earned her the nickname "Oozy Isobol."

It didn't kill her. But it did humble her. She resigned from any further revenge spells, especially those having to do with affairs of the heart. Since her lover had been a married man, she essentially cursed herself since she was his mistress long before he added a second to the mix. The universe would dole out justice the way it saw fit.

"No. Not at all. I'm thinking it's probably just a topical fungus," Aunt Astrid said pleasantly.

"Do you want to tell me why you can't seem to leave my family alone?" Fern hissed while she scribbled on the clipboard of my aunt's paperwork.

"What do you mean?" Aunt Astrid said, playing dumb.

"I know who you are, Mrs. Greenstone. You show up at my mother's funeral, trying to get information from my sister. You crash my house to try to talk to my father. Now you have your other family member snooping around my sister's veterinarian office just like you are doing here." Fern clenched her teeth. "What is it that you think you are doing?"

"Fern, please," Bea interrupted. "You've got it all wrong. It's just a happy coincidence we keep running into you guys. That's all."

"A happy coincidence?" she snapped bitterly. "This is my practice. This entire building is mine, and I'm telling you to leave. Do not come back, or there will be severe consequences."

It was at this time that the shadow people started getting more visible to Aunt Astrid. One stood at the door Fern had walked through, and the other was immediately to Fern's left.

"They were like bouncers," Bea said. "I tried to

act innocent with Fern and reached out to touch her arm. You would have thought I tried to stick her with a used needle. She slapped my hand away and—"

"Slapped your hand away?" I gasped.

"Literally." Bea nodded with her eyes wide, showing as much shock as me. "I was going to make an issue of it, but Mom took hold of my hand and started to pull me toward the door. Tell her what you saw, Mom."

I looked at my aunt, whose forehead was a sea of wrinkles as she thought about what she saw.

"It was like the place was decaying. Like how a person films a flower growing from seed to bloom and it is sped up for the camera. That was how this looked. I could see it, but Bea couldn't."

My cousin shook her head again.

According to my aunt, the paint and plaster began to peel and crumble. Cobwebs and grime began to form and spread out from the corners. The floor began to fade underneath a bed of dirt and strange dark patches where water or some other kind of ooze had seeped up from the ground.

"How did you get out of there?" I stroked Treacle's fur as he slunk around my leg before plopping down on the floor to nap.

"For a second, I didn't think we were going to make it," my aunt continued.

She and Bea continued to apologize to Fern, who was watching them with an icy stare. But it was obvious their cover had been blown, and any unnecessary lingering might cause more harm than good. As Fern took a step closer to Aunt Astrid, so did the shadow that was at her side.

"I reached for the doorknob, and when I took hold of it, I felt a frigid, slimy coating. There was nothing there that I could see, but I felt it. It made my hand slip. Bea and I could feel those shadows closing in on us. The air was getting thicker. I tasted a mossy dampness in my mouth. Finally, I was able to get a strong enough grip to wrench the door open."

Bea let her breath out as if making a sound might change the outcome of their experience. "We walked out into the waiting room, and several of the people who had been waiting when we arrived stood up and began to approach us," she said.

"Like the rat man at the vet," I mumbled.

"Yeah. They were all big, and their features were dark. But not like Jake's are dark. These weren't people. They looked like people at first, but if you stared at them, you could see their skin sinking into their bones and murky shadows settling into every fold and crevice. There were four of them in the lobby. We were the only ones who could see them."

"What happened once you got outside?" I asked.

"Well, we thanked our lucky stars for the bright sunshine and the cold temperature that snapped us back into this reality," my aunt said. "We got in the car and sped home."

"I don't mean to sound negative," Bea said as she poured her mom some more tea, "but I have no idea what we should do now."

"Neither do I," I added. "But if those circled dates on the calendar in Gail's office are what I think they are, we don't have a lot of time. Another member of the Elderflower family is going to die."

"Cath is right," Aunt Astrid replied. "First things first. Tomorrow, we need to stop by the apothecary. I need sage and lots of it. We've got to clean Cath's house before we even think of trying to help the Elderflowers. We'll also need to pool our strength, so Bea, anything you can cook up that will give us that extra physical boost is what we need."

"Sure. Cath will love it. Avocado. Spinach. Maybe even some tofu for good measure," Bea teased. She knew I hated when we had to force vitamins. But if it meant never seeing that shadow creature in my bedroom ever again, I'd choke down a raw turnip.

"Cath, you'll need to get the cats up to speed. We're going to need them, especially if Treacle scared away the one in your bedroom. There has to be something about the felines that these creatures don't like. We've got three. We'd be silly not to get them involved."

"What are *you* going to do?" I asked.

My aunt looked at Bea and me.

"I'm going to ask an old friend for some help."

Bea and I had no idea what Aunt Astrid was talking about. We didn't know what old friend or what they could possibly add to the situation. But we trusted she knew what she was doing.

Since I was still staying at my aunt's house, I walked outside with Bea as she made the journey three doors down to her house.

"Flip the porch light twice so I know you are inside behind a locked door," I ordered.

"Yeah. I will. Then you run back inside. I don't care how silly you think it looks," she said as she started walking backward toward her home.

"I will."

Bea did as she was told and flipped the porch light twice. I was about to do what I was told when I saw a light go on across the street. That was my house. It was supposed to be empty. But a shadow passed in front of the window.

I didn't plan on going in. I was only going to peek through the windows and then call the cops. But when I stepped on the porch and the front door opened, I stepped in to investigate. I knew it was stupid. But I did it anyway. I thought I'd regret it until the day I died.

## 17

### COMBAT BOOTS

"Cath! Cath, wake up! Please wake up!"

I heard Aunt Astrid's voice, but it sounded far off. I was lying down. I knew that. It felt painless and comfortable. For a minute, I was sure my head was detached from my body because I couldn't feel a thing. I wanted to slip back into that void of deep, deep sleep and catch a few more z's. I didn't want to talk or move or even sit up.

"Cath! Come on! Open your eyes! Open them!"

That was when the cold settled in. Nothing ruined sleep like being cold and not having a heavy enough blanket. I thought I reached down to pull up my covers, but it was only in my mind. I didn't feel the mattress underneath me. In fact, my hipbone was starting to ache as it poked into the hard concrete floor. When I opened my eyes, everything was twisted sideways. I was on the floor in my basement.

Treacle's window was open just enough for the cat to squeeze through.

"Cath? Can you hear me? Nod if you can," my aunt said. Just then, I heard heavy footsteps coming down the steps.

"Is she okay?"

It was Tom. Oh no. The last thing I wanted was for him to see me like this. I blinked and focused and painfully pushed myself up.

"I'm okay."

"You are not," Aunt Astrid barked. "You've got a gash over your head, and you may not have broken your ankle, but it is severely twisted. Don't move. Bea is on her way."

"What happened? Why am I in the basement?"

"I was hoping you could tell me that," Tom said as he rushed up to my side.

"What happened to you?" I asked.

"I was coming by to bring you something. I saw you come into the house. But when I got to the door, it was locked tight. I rang the doorbell and knocked. Nothing. I started to shout for you, and that was when your aunt came from across the street."

I looked at my aunt. All the worry in her face made me sad, and I tried to sit up, but my head began to pound. When I reached up, I felt my hair was wet. I knew it was blood, but I wasn't going to look.

"She waited at the front door, and I went around back. That was when I saw your back door had been pried open. I pulled out my gun, and just as I started searching the place, calling your name, a dark figure dashed toward the front door and ran out."

"Did you see who it was?" I looked at my aunt.

She licked her lips nervously.

"All I saw was a person with long black hair and black clothing. She had a hood pulled far down over her face. Combat boots."

"Evelyn?" I was in shock.

"Like I said, honey. I couldn't see her face." I could tell by my aunt's voice that the answer was yes but she just didn't want to tell me. "Tom flipped on all the lights, and the door to your basement was open. I told him I'd look for you. He took off after the girl."

"Yeah. But a lot of good that did. I'm not sure where she ran off to, but I lost her quickly. It was like she just vanished."

"Mom!" Bea yelled from upstairs.

"Down here, Bea!" my aunt called back.

"I'm going to search upstairs. I'll be back in a minute," Tom said as he quickly went back up the steps and held the door back for Bea.

"Why did you come in here when Mom told you not to?" she scolded me.

"I saw a shadow moving around," I admitted. It sounded as dumb an excuse as it was. "This is my house, after all."

"But Mom told you it needed to be smudged. Don't you ever listen?" Bea's bottom lip trembled as tears filled her eyes. "You can be so selfish sometimes, Cath Greenstone!"

My cousin had never spoken to me like that. I looked up at my aunt, who was still holding me against her. But I was surprised when her eyes didn't meet mine.

The lump in my throat forced out the words I would have never said on my own.

"I'm sorry." It wasn't that I thought I was always right. I didn't. But when I did something wrong or impulsive, saying "I'm sorry" always seemed a little lame. It was easier to take some of Bea's chores at the diner so she could go home early or pick up some supplies for Aunt Astrid that she wasn't expecting in order to save her a trip. Actions spoke louder than words, right?

"You should be sorry." Bea rubbed her hands together and sniffled. "What would I do without you? You're my sister. Do you think I want to lose you to a monster under the bed?"

The words pierced my heart. That was how my mom died. Now my eyes filled with tears. I felt my aunt's arms around me squeeze me affectionately.

"Lay her down, Mom," Bea ordered. "Just to teach you a lesson, I'm going to go put my hands in your freezer for a couple seconds."

As my aunt helped me lie flat on the cold concrete floor, I took her hand in my left hand and Bea's hand in my right. I couldn't find the words, so I just squeezed as a couple tears fell.

"Okay. I need you to lie still. Just let me have a look at you." Bea smiled through her own tears. I watched her face become serious as she inspected not my physical skull and neck but all the little areas where energy travelled. It was as if she were combing for lice. She poked and prodded through every fiber of my aura, looking for some sign of serious blockage. Her hands held my face, my shoulders, and my arms and ran through my hair. When she got to my ankle, I saw her eyebrows purse together.

"There isn't a break, but you'll be gimpy for a while."

"Did you just call me gimpy? Not all that politically correct, are you?" I huffed through the pain of Bea touching my ankle.

"Oh, when you bring trouble on yourself like you did, you just wait. If you think gimpy is bad, you're going to hate it when I refer to you as Cath the Cripple."

Even Aunt Astrid had to chuckle.

"I'm glad you two are finding so much humor at my expense."

"Hush and stay still," Bea ordered. I couldn't see anything, but Bea continued to run her hands over the length of my body. Even through the pain in my ankle, I could feel her encouraging my inner energies to flow and circulate more than they usually did. My fingertips and toes tingled, and my head began to clear and stop aching.

"Okay." Bea sat back on her heels. "I think you'll live. Mom, does her head need stitches?"

"I don't think so." Aunt Astrid looked at the side of my head and then at my face. "But you'll want to be careful brushing your hair. Let's get you back across the street. This place is starting to get heavy. Do you feel it?"

"I do," Bea admitted.

Before I could push myself up off the floor, Bea had called for Tom.

"No. I can make it up the stairs," I protested.

"Hey, you can argue all you want, but your aunt isn't going to let you get up any other way," Tom said. "I've got to carry you. It isn't up to me, Cath. Aunt Astrid is the boss."

I looked at my aunt, who had a stern look on her face. As much as I hated to admit it, Tom was right. There was no telling Aunt Astrid no.

"This is humiliating," I muttered in Tom's ear.

"Really? I think it's kind of romantic."

"Pay attention to the stairs and where you are going." I harrumphed.

Once we were out of the basement, Bea held the front door open, and Aunt Astrid put a camouflage spell on the broken back door. If anyone decided to go snooping around or if the intruder decided to come back, they would see a plank of plywood over the entire door. If they tried to remove it, a shock of electricity would be sent through them. That worked as a deterrent as well as an alarm directly to Aunt Astrid.

Once we were safely at Aunt Astrid's house, Bea helped me take a bath while my aunt told Tom about the old friend she was going to be contacting for some help.

When I finally came downstairs, I knew I looked a mess. I had on my aunt's baggy flannel pajamas that were wonderfully warm and cozy but not what you'd want your boyfriend to see you in. My hair was wet, and I had a big, goofy Band-Aid along my hairline.

My aunt was packing Tom a small snack of chocolate pie, half a turkey sandwich from the café, a bag of homemade potato chips, an apple, and a plastic container of cheese squares and crackers.

"I was on my way to work when I stopped by. I've got to get going now."

"Sorry you had to deal with all that," I said.

"Well, whoever was there was lying in wait for you."

"How do you know?" I shivered and looked at my aunt and Bea, who were both listening.

"Some of the things you keep under your bed were pushed out. Also, there was a knife from your cutting block lying on the floor. They must have dropped it when I came in."

I was afraid I was going to puke. The lump in my throat wouldn't go down when I swallowed.

"What a mess." I gulped.

"What do you mean? I got to carry you in my arms. The night turned out better than I had imagined."

I blushed all over the place and wanted to melt into the floor. The lump in my throat gave way to butterflies in my stomach. I smiled at him and enjoyed a long kiss good night.

"If you two are finished, I've got to get back home too. Jake will be very worried when I tell him what happened. But I think since this was a person we know, Jake should be put on alert."

"Tom, would you make sure Bea gets home okay?" I asked as I opened the front door.

"Of course."

"You," Bea growled. "Get some rest. Don't go anywhere. Treacle and Marshmallow will sleep with you. That ought to help keep your circulation going. By tomorrow, you should feel good except for that ankle. It might take a few days to right itself."

I nodded. There was no way I was going to put up a fight.

After they were gone and I locked the door, I hobbled up to my aunt.

"So, what do you think about this?"

"I can't think anymore." She rubbed her eyes. "I'm going to have one last cup of tea, and then I might take a catnap. You should go to bed. Take my room."

I didn't argue. Instead, I gave my aunt a kiss on the cheek and hopped pitifully to bed. Treacle and Marshmallow were there and did exactly what Bea had said they would. Treacle perched around my head, and Marshmallow curled up at my feet. There was a constant flow of energy back and forth that was warm and sedating. Almost instantly, I fell into a deep sleep. But it didn't last. When I woke up, only about an hour had passed, and my aunt was still up.

I crept out of the bed, hoping for a glass of water and maybe a forkful of pie. But I heard my aunt talking quietly. At first, I thought she was chanting a spell or something. But then I heard her laugh. It wasn't the kind of laugh as if she'd seen something funny on television. This was a giggle like a girl who was being flirted with.

I tiptoed to her study and carefully peeked in.

"Oh, my love. If only you were here with me. We'd have so much fun on these adventures. The girls have grown into such beautiful women. Bea has your eyes. Your niece definitely has the Greenstone sense of humor."

I could hear whispers replying to my aunt, but they were so low I couldn't make out any words.

"I hate this time had to be wasted on this problem. But I'm scared for the girls. Thank you for your help. Until next year, then, my love."

Quietly, I slipped back to the bedroom and climbed under the covers to the nonstop purring motors of the cats. I barely noticed the throbbing in my ankle as I thought about the calendar.

"What day is it?" I scrolled through the week and month, coming to February 6. It was a Tuesday. "It's the worm moon." I snapped my fingers and slapped my head only to wince. The worm moon was also called the Lenten moon or Crow moon. It was the last full moon before the vernal equinox. It was the one night out of the year that a witch could call the name of a deceased loved one, or in some cases a desperately hated rival, and speak with them. A witch could communicate with the dead at any time of the year, but it resulted in severe energy draining. It often required more than one day to recuperate. The Worm moon was like a freebie.

Just then, I realized who it was my aunt was talking to. Uncle Eagle Eye.

## 18

### THE APOTHECARY

The next morning, other than a slight headache, I was feeling pretty good. Until I put my foot on the floor and tried to walk.

"Yeow!" I hollered. "Oh, this is going to be great at work."

At that moment, I heard feet pounding toward my room. I knew they were moving too fast to be my aunt's. It had to be Bea's.

"Good morning, spaz," she chirped cheerily.

"Good morning. Would you get a load of this ankle? It looks like a grapefruit in a pair of pantyhose."

"Ha! It does," she replied.

Peanut Butter slunk in the room and hopped up

on the bed with Treacle and Marshmallow, who were slowly stretching themselves awake.

"The gang's all here." I gave them each a scratch under the chin. "I don't know what I'm going to do about work. How am I going to get around with this?"

"Well, Jake had a splendid idea. It's waiting for you downstairs."

"Jake? Had an idea? I don't want it."

"You don't even know what it is."

"Doesn't matter. Let's just say sympathy isn't Jake's strongest asset."

"Well, you did bring this on yourself." Bea chewed her nail daintily. "And you did make Mom and me worry terribly. Not to mention poor Tom having to lug you upstairs after giving chase to the intruder."

"Evelyn," I answered.

"Maybe? From the description, probably," she said, frowning.

We sat there for a moment.

"I overheard your mom last night. She was talking to your dad." I wasn't sure if I should be telling Bea, but it didn't feel right to keep it to myself.

"She was? Are you sure?"

"Yeah. I could tell by what she was saying." I cleared my throat. "She told him how pretty you are and how funny I am. That he'd be proud of us."

Bea looked at her nails.

"I don't remember too much about my dad," Bea admitted. "He died when we were little."

"I don't remember too much either," I admitted. "But I remember him being a nice man. Apples don't fall far from the tree." I gave her a gentle nudge with my elbow.

"I wonder why she reached over to the other side like that. Mom doesn't usually like to dive too deep into those dimensions. She prefers to stay local, so to speak."

"I think she was asking for his opinion on the Elderflower situation. We had an actual person break into my house yesterday. The police are completely capable of handling that. But the Gazzo and his crew —I don't know. Well, let's go to the kitchen." I slipped my arm through Bea's. "Let's see what Jake's idea of helping is."

As we hobbled to the kitchen, I was overwhelmed with gratitude for the family I had. For all our weirdness and dramatic history, not to mention the adventures we stumbled upon, I would never want a normal life. To be like everyone else would be to not be a Greenstone.

"Oh heck no!" I shouted when I saw Jake's "gift."

"Surprise!" he yelled with a cup of coffee in his hand. "We had this in our lost and found at the station for about a year. No one came to claim it, so consider it yours."

"I am not using a walker. With tennis balls on the legs, to boot." I tried to sound angry, but I wanted to laugh.

"That's not all," Jake said. "Blake, give her the other part."

My chest constricted as I heard Jake call Blake. I should have known he'd be here too. These two partners were rarely separated for long. I didn't know how Bea could stand it.

"Hope you feel better soon, Cath." Blake said as he handed me a gift bag. I peeked inside and frowned.

"You guys think you are really funny." I rolled my eyes.

"What is it?" Aunt Astrid asked.

"Yeah, don't keep it all to yourself." Bea urged, but I could tell from her face that she already knew what it was.

I reached in the bag and pulled out one of those

old-fashioned honking horns. It had a black rubber ball on one end and a wide-mouthed horn on the other end.

"Here." Jake took it from my hand. He was grinning from ear to ear.

"You are really enjoying this way too much," I said.

"You can attach it right on the top part. Or maybe it would be better closer to your hand." He fastened it onto my walker and stood back proudly. "There. Looks great! Give it a try!"

"I'm not honking this horn."

"Cath, don't be a party pooper," Bea said.

Reluctantly, I gave the black rubber ball a squeeze.

*Hwwwaaa. Hwwwaaa.*

The entire kitchen erupted in laughter. Except, Blake, of course. He didn't laugh. But he grinned. That was as far as he'd let his hair down.

Sadly, I found the walker to be quite helpful. It was a little awkward. The idea of going out in public with it was embarrassing. Bea refused to let me take the horn off. But I couldn't stay home. Not when we had so much work to do.

After Jake and Blake got their morning funnies at my expense, they left for work. Aunt Astrid had made a simple breakfast of oatmeal with fresh berries. As much as I tried to stay away from fresh fruits and veggies, I gobbled it up as if it were my last meal on death row.

Aunt Astrid was going to open up the café and take care of that while Bea and I went shopping. We had a list of things we needed to get from The Apothecary on the other side of town. After that, we were to come right back to the café. But so often, things didn't turn out the way we planned.

"I love the smell of this store," Bea said as we walked into The Apothecary.

Mimi Van Doss was the proprietor. She had absolutely no witch blood running through her veins, but that didn't stop her from dressing the part. She was also an encyclopedia on stones, herbs, flowers, candles, and half a dozen other things that I didn't even know were witchy. She often helped us with materials we needed for our spells and never asked any questions. She was worth her weight in gold, if you asked me. And that would be a lot of gold.

"Hey, Bea! Hey, Cath! Where have you two been hiding yourselves?" Mimi maneuvered her voluptuous figure out from behind the counter to give us both hugs. "What happened to you?" She gasped as she looked at the walker. As I feared, she grabbed the horn and gave a squeeze.

*Hwwwaaa. Hwwwaaa.*

"It's a long story." I rolled my eyes.

"She had a break-in at her house." Bea folded her arms across her chest. I looked at her. Was she really going to tell everyone what happened? "You may as well be honest, Cath. Everyone is going to ask you."

"Either that or make up a different story for every person who asks," Mimi suggested, giggling. She wore tight corsets that pushed everything up and out in all directions, so when she laughed, there was a lot of jiggling. But as long as she looked like the stereotypical image of a witch, people were less likely to look at the Greenstones. "Tell one person you lost a wrestling match with a crocodile. Tell the next person you tried out for the Oakland Raiders. Tell another you fell rock climbing."

"That's a good idea." I smiled and felt genuinely better. "You sure do have a way of putting a positive spin on things, Mimi."

"I do my best. So, what are you guys looking for today?"

The Apothecary was known for having wonderful-smelling soaps and bath crystals. A shopper could find aspirin, cold medicine, and shampoos as well. Mimi also sold beautifully designed talismans, semi-precious stones, and jar after jar of herbs and spices ranging from achiote seed to za'atar and everything in between.

But in her special back room for special customers, she had live crickets, tarantulas, snake skins, dried bat wings, and toads, along with special bundles of sage, cornhusks, and hemlock.

"All of my animal products were obtained humanely, and not a single animal was killed by me or my provider in order to acquire them. Just so you know." she'd told us the first time we came into the store.

"Mimi, we need some of your very best sage," Bea said as she pulled Aunt Astrid's list from her coat pocket. As she read off each item, I started to roll myself along the aisles, looking for something that might be nice for Tom. He had carried me up those stairs, and Valentine's Day was coming up. I owed him.

"Cath, I'm going in the back with Mimi. I'll be right back."

*Hwwwaaa. Hwwwaaa.*

I heard her laugh and then couldn't help but chuckle myself.

While I was standing in the aisle with men's

cologne, I heard the chimes over the door tinkle. There was no reason for me to pay any attention to it until I saw the two heads of thick dyed-black hair coming in my direction.

They must have known what was in the back room too, because that was where they were headed. I decided to follow. It was difficult to be tough with a walker, but I was determined.

"Hey. Looking for something?" I barked. "A crowbar? Or maybe a lock-picking kit?"

Evelyn whirled around. She had been crying, but when she looked at me, she smiled until she saw the walker.

"What happened?" She gasped, quickly wiping her cheeks.

"How could you break into my house? You and your friend aren't going anywhere. I'm calling the police."

"Break into your house? What are you talking about?"

"Evelyn, my boyfriend saw you, and so did my aunt. Did you really think you could just break into my place and push me down the stairs and get away with it?"

I leaned on my walker and tried to look threatening, but it wasn't working.

"Cath, I didn't break into your house. I'd never do that. Not to you or anyone."

"But they saw you. Are you calling my boyfriend and my aunt liars?"

"What did they see? And when? When did this happen?" Her eyes began to water, and she sniffled. "I'm tired of being blamed for everything! I didn't do it! Go ahead and call the cops, and when they check my alibi, you'll see how wrong you are! You are no different from Fern and Ga—"

She cut herself off and looked around nervously.

The three of us stood there in silence for a few seconds.

"This happened last night, Evelyn. Around seven or maybe eight o'clock."

"I was at home. Heather was with me as well as my father. We watched the original *Star Wars* and then did our homework, and Heather left around eleven. Go ahead. Check it out." Evelyn wiped her eyes again.

"She's telling you the truth," her friend Heather said, putting a hand on Evelyn's shoulder. "Look, we might look scary, but we would never break into anyone's house. This isn't really who we are."

Maybe it was because I had the same kinds of issues in high school as Evelyn did, but I couldn't help feeling she was telling the truth. I looked down, and that was when I saw her feet. She was wearing a pair of black canvas shoes.

"Where are your combat boots? It's freezing outside."

"I can't find them." She sniffled.

Whoever broke into my house had been wearing combat boots.

My whole body slumped.

"Evelyn, are you and Heather supposed to be in school?"

They looked nervously at each other.

"I'm not going to turn you in. I'm hoping you'll come with me back to the café." My strong leg was getting tired, but putting any pressure on my swollen ankle made me wince and clench my teeth.

"I've got straight As," Evelyn offered. "So does Heather. We find it very therapeutic to skip school once in a while. If we didn't refill the well every so often, we'd probably start to fail our courses."

I squinted at them.

"Refill the well? Okay. Can you come with Bea and me and spend a little time with us?"

"Okay, but we won't be able to stay too long," she said sadly.

"Why? A prior commitment or some Goth-Vampira convention to go to?"

"No." Evelyn didn't laugh. "They come looking for me if I stay in one place too long."

"Who does?"

Evelyn tried not to cry.

"The shadow people."

## 19

## LOAN SHARKS

When Bea finally appeared with Mimi, it was as if she had been shopping for Christmas. Her arms were full of bundles and bags, her eyes were twinkling with excitement, and she was grinning insanely.

"Well, Mimi, it looks like my cousin made sure you have money for your bills for the next couple of months," I chided.

"What is she doing here?" Bea asked, looking directly at Evelyn. "Have you called the police? I'm calling Jake. She's not going to get away this time."

"Calm down, Bea. Please."

"This is serious. You could have died last night." She scowled at Evelyn. "Do you have any idea what you've done?"

"Bea." I put my hand on my cousin's arm.

"Evelyn is coming to the café with us. Heather too. We're going to have a nice long talk."

Bea set down her packages on the counter and mumbled under her breath. Poor Mimi had no idea what was happening. Her big brown eyes bounced from me to Bea to Evelyn to Heather and back to me again.

"Ring us up, Mimi. We've got to get going."

"Fine. But if you hooligans are coming with us, you're carrying the bags. And don't even think of running off with them. I was all-star track in school. I'll grab one of you and drag you to the police myself."

I looked at Bea without expression. Not only was she not all-star track, but she didn't play any sports. I didn't think she'd run even if she were being chased.

The girls were quiet as they piled into the back of my beater. I wasn't driving.

"Strap yourselves in, girls. Bea might hit thirty miles an hour because she's upset." I smirked at my cousin.

Evelyn and Heather chuckled.

"It's true. Get those belts tight."

"Ha. You are so funny. Hilarious." Bea grumbled, watching the girls in the rearview mirror.

Finally, after a fifteen-minute drive that took twenty-five minutes, everyone got out of the car and hurried into the café.

"You really are a very slow driver," Heather said as she took all the bags Bea piled into her arms.

"Shut up and get inside," Bea growled.

Thankfully, the café was empty.

"Would you girls take those packages and set them down on that table in the back? Don't worry. I'll make sure you are safe here."

They both nodded and went into the secluded area of the café where Aunt Astrid usually did her private palm or tarot readings.

"Aunt Astrid, can you throw up a smoke screen?"

"What do you mean?"

"Evelyn said that she can't stay in one place too long, or they'll find her."

"Is she talking about her sister?"

"No. She said the shadow people."

Bea froze as she was hanging up her coat and looked at me. Aunt Astrid narrowed her eyes and bit her bottom lip.

"How would she know about the shadow people unless she saw them too?" I whispered. "And why are they bothering her? You said that those things were like loan sharks. I don't get the impression that

Evelyn took out any loan. She doesn't even know what she's dealing with. She's got to be able to stop and catch her breath. It's the only way we'll be able to figure out what is going on."

My aunt took a deep breath. After dumping a shaker of salt into her hand, she walked along the perimeter of the café and sprinkled the granules around. She whispered her spell and then pulled down a jar of sage used for cooking. She took out a pinch and told Evelyn to stand up.

"Put this in your pocket," she ordered Evelyn. "You too, toots," she said to Heather.

Once again, both girls did as they were told without question.

"This is screwy," Heather said.

"Just do it," Evelyn said, not wanting to look impolite.

She was really quite naïve when it came to street smarts. Heather at least called it as she saw it. She was obviously a bit tougher than her friend. But Evelyn was truly good. I could sense it. But someone out there wanted her to be bad. Or at least to look as if she were.

"Okay. I'd say we've got an hour, maybe less," Aunt Astrid said to me. We looked at the girls as if we were deciding on a turkey at the grocery store.

"Bea. Why don't you start?"

"Start what?" Evelyn asked.

"The torture," I replied seriously.

I got the exact response I wanted. Both girls frowned and looked at each other.

"I'm joking. Bea is just going to bring you some tea, and when she's done, you are going to hand the cups over to my aunt, and she's going to read them. In the meantime, who wants cake?"

"You know how to read tea leaves?" Evelyn's voice shook a little.

"I do. My mother taught me," Aunt Astrid said as she took her usual seat at the table. "Did your mother teach you anything special while you were growing up?" Aunt Astrid's voice was soft and kind. I remember hearing that tone many times when I cried over my mother.

"She taught me how to knit." Evelyn instantly choked up.

"That's wonderful." Aunt Astrid let the girl cry. "That's one of those gifts that you can use for pleasure and profit. The best kind of thing a mother can teach her daughter." She looked at Heather. "What about you?"

"I can cook. Do laundry. Nothing special."

"Are you kidding? Do you know how many grown

men don't know how to do those things? To a fellow worth his salt, that will be heaven-sent. Don't short-change yourself."

Bea brought the tea just as the girls were cozying up to Aunt Astrid. I hobbled behind my walker and looked at the cakes underneath the glass domes on the counter.

"When did Kevin make this?" I tried to keep my excitement low, but there was a maple coconut yellow cake with a cherry on top just sitting there without a single slice taken out. Quickly, I cut three pieces and put them on plates. That was when I heard the laughter. Using the counter to move, I leaned away from the walker and peeked around the corner. Bea was holding Evelyn's hand while Heather was telling a story about a boy she liked.

Bea looked up at me and smiled. It was obvious she had seen something in Evelyn's aura that was a little more tangible than last time. And if I knew Bea, she absorbed some of the girl's pain over the loss of her mother. Bea was terribly compassionate that way.

"Help with the cake?" I looked at Bea, but Evelyn jumped up and came around the counter. "Thanks."

"This looks good," she said.

"Kevin, our baker, is amazing. Wait until you taste it."

I hovered around the counter because my gift of telepathy with the animals wasn't needed at this juncture. I left the pros to handle these girls for the time being, and I listened very carefully.

Heather finished her tea first, so my aunt took a look.

"Heather, you have a tendency to speak your mind, and it often gets you in trouble." Aunt Astrid didn't look up as she spoke.

"Sometimes," the girl said proudly.

"You also have a natural gift around animals. They trust you. You've had encounters with birds and raccoons and... what is this? Oh, a pit bull. They came to you for help, and you helped them."

She gasped. "The pit bull is Roxy. I got her from the pound. They said they were going to put her down because no one wanted her. She was a bit of a runt."

"That dog will be at your side for many, many years. As long as she's with you, she'll never let anything happen to you. She knows you saved her life."

I heard the sniffles and casually wiped the

counter in order to turn around and see Heather wiping her eyes with a napkin.

"I'd look into a career as a vet if I were you. Studying comes naturally. Veterinary school should be a walk in the park." Aunt Astrid winked. "Now, how about you?" She focused intently on Evelyn's leaves. I leaned against the counter with my bum ankle raised and watched, waiting for the same enthusiastic reading as Heather got. But Aunt Astrid's expression fell. Something was wrong.

"Evelyn, you've got a heavy burden on your shoulders. It's weighing on you all the time, isn't it?"

She didn't say anything.

"You can talk about it here," my aunt said soothingly. "You're among friends."

Evelyn swallowed hard, and sweat started to break out on her forehead.

"They might hear me."

"Who, honey?"

"If they hear me, they'll tell my sisters," she whispered. "My dad will be in trouble."

"I can assure you, Evelyn, no one will hear what you say in this café. And nothing you say will be repeated." The authority in Aunt Astrid's voice was something Bea and I learned about long ago. She told the truth.

Evelyn looked at Bea and me and then Aunt Astrid.

"My sisters aren't right," she muttered. "They've done something. Bad. And they don't plan on stopping."

"What did they do?" Aunt Astrid asked.

Evelyn looked nervously around and past me to the front of the café.

"I don't have any proof. You're going to think I'm crazy. But they aren't smart enough to be doctors." Evelyn sighed as if she'd just revealed a huge secret.

"What do you mean?" I asked.

"They got help," she continued.

"Honey, you aren't making any sense," Aunt Astrid said soothingly. "Do you know what she means?" She looked at Heather.

"All I know is that as long as I've known Evelyn, her sisters have been mean to her. Right?" She looked at her friend. "It's just jealousy. Evelyn is prettier than they are and most definitely smarter. They hate her for that."

"Is this true?" Bea sat down next to Evelyn and placed her hand on her forearm.

"Partly," Evelyn admitted. She kept looking around as if she were waiting for a bus. She swallowed hard and put her other hand on Bea's. I was sure she could feel strength there. I kept my fingers crossed it would be enough to get her to tell us something more. "They did something. Something with a Ouija board."

*Now we're getting somewhere.*

I could tell by my aunt's body language that this made her mad. It was a simple thing. People had been told not to play with Ouija boards since the things were invented, and yet they continued to do so. Then they wondered why their lives fell apart.

"What did they do?" Bea asked.

"They made some kind of deal." Evelyn was speaking more confidently. "They told me my days were numbered and that no one would miss me. That no one would be left to miss me."

It broke my heart to watch her sitting there. She cried like a little girl, and the makeup on her face ran down her cheeks. Heather put her arm around her. She also had tears in her eyes.

"You calm down now, honey." Aunt Astrid's voice was firm. "We can help. But we need to keep being brave for just a little while longer."

"If you say anything to them, they'll get mad!" Evelyn croaked. "They have some kind of power. They're witches or something."

"Honey, they aren't witches." Aunt Astrid said

that with such conviction I wanted to cheer. I looked at Bea, who was reading my mind.

We let the girls stay at the café for the rest of the afternoon. It was a windy day, and the foot traffic was pretty low. I told Bea and my aunt about Evelyn losing her boots and her alibi for last night. Everything was starting to point to another person breaking into my house, and I was feeling pretty confident we all knew who it was. Or at least had it narrowed down to two people.

"So what do we do?" Bea asked Aunt Astrid quietly as we prepared the girls some healthy spinach-and-turkey salads with a cranberry dressing Bea concocted.

"After they've finished eating, you girls should drive them home. See what there is to see around Evelyn's house. Then get back here as quickly as you can. I'll be getting our supplies ready. Girls, we are going to have teach the Elderflowers a lesson."

## 20

## THREE HUMAN FORMS

E velyn and Heather were in much better spirits as we drove them home.

"Are you sure your mom won't mind you staying at Evelyn's house? We can get you to your front door, no problem," Bea said.

"We were going to hang out after school anyway. My mom is working late tonight at the Dollar General, so she doesn't mind. My dad is on a three-day job. He's a truck driver."

"That makes me feel better that you guys are sticking together," I said, turning around from the front seat. "Is your dad home, Evelyn?"

"I don't know. Fern and Gail have been forcing him to look at old folks' homes even though he only just turned sixty. They keep telling him he's too old to take care of me."

If I didn't have a bad ankle, I would have stopped at the sporting goods store, picked up a Louisville Slugger, and waited for those two witchy wannabes to get home. Then I would have taught them a lesson about respecting their elders and not playing with Ouija boards.

But I did have a bum ankle, and I was so bad at sports that I'd probably crack my own skull before cracking anyone else's.

When we pulled up in front of Evelyn's house, the girls hopped out.

"Cath, I'm sorry about your ankle," Evelyn said after I rolled my window down.

"It's okay, kid. It'll heal." I smiled.

"I'm afraid to go in the house," she confided. "For the first time in a long time, I felt safe at your café. It was like the feeling of coming up from underwater."

"And now?"

"I feel like I'm being watched again. I can see them out of the corners of my eyes, but when I look, nothing is there." She growled. "One thing is different. I don't feel as scared."

"Good. Here. This is from Aunt Astrid. Get a big plate, and burn it. Let the smoke go all around your room. It'll help calm you."

"What is it?"

"Just a little sage. My aunt swears by it."

Evelyn took the bundle of sage. She and Heather went into the house and waved from the window, smiling.

"Do you think they'll be okay?" I asked Bea.

"I hope so. Do you see that?" She pointed to the side of the house that was casting a long shadow as the sun was starting to go down.

I squinted. Was I seeing things right?

"I don't believe it," I grumbled. From the shadow emerged three human forms. They were barely there and just a shade darker than the rest of the natural shadow on the ground. If you weren't looking for them, you wouldn't see anything more than something out of the corner of your eye. But Bea and I knew they were around. We could see them. They could see us.

"Is the one in the middle wearing a hat?" I asked. The whole idea of a shadow person wearing a hat annoyed me. It was as if the thing were trying to be cool, as if being a shadow person weren't scary enough, but one of them had to don a human element. I was freaked out and annoyed all at once.

"It sure looks like it. Unless its head is shaped like that," Bea answered.

"I don't think its head is shaped like a top hat. That's just crazy."

"Right." Bea scowled. "I'm scared. Do you think we should get Evelyn and Heather?"

"No." I listened to my instincts. "Those things are ready to pounce on us, but I don't think Evelyn and Heather are in any danger. Not from these guys, anyway."

"If you say so."

For the first time ever, Bea threw the car in reverse, spun out of the driveway, and put the hammer down. We got back to the café in ten minutes when it normally took half an hour.

"Remind me not to tease you about your driving anymore." I clutched my heart. "Good thing those lights were yellow when you sped through them. I just hope Jake doesn't get hold of the photos from the cameras that caught his wife breaking the law."

"It's your car. You are the one who'll get the tickets," she sassed.

As I pulled myself out of the car, Bea ran to the front door to hold it open. I shuffled as fast as I could because it was terribly cold and because every shadow seemed as though it were moving behind me and gaining.

"Lock the doors, girls. We're closing early."

I was so happy to hear those words I almost giggled. Evelyn was right. It felt safe at the café.

"Should I shut the lights off?" I asked.

"No!" Aunt Astrid shouted. "No. After you girls left, I did a little digging based on what Evelyn told us combined with the mutilation of her mother's corpse and the strange claim that the Elderflower girls made a deal. They did. And I'm afraid to say 'with Satan' might be a slight understatement."

My stomach soured. Nothing sounded scarier than the words *devil* or *demonic* except *Satan* or something worse than Satan. What did these idiots get us into?

Under the bright lights of the café, Aunt Astrid plopped down the *Greenstone Lexicon*. It was one of the older reference books she had in her arsenal. Within its delicate pages, she stuck a couple of red Valentine's Day napkins to hold her places.

"If these aren't what we're dealing with, then this might be like taking a knife to a gunfight."

"What?" I swallowed.

"We're in this now, Mom. You know you can count on us."

"We will have to get the cats. Treacle was able to fend one off Cath. There's no telling how many will be there by now."

"But where? How many what?" I asked. "And about this knife to a gunfight thing. That's just a figure of speech, right? You don't really mean we'll be outgunned, do you?"

"At the Elderflowers' house. The shadow people," Aunt Astrid said. "And yes. If I'm wrong about this, we might have no other option than to run and keep running."

My cousin patted me on the shoulder and smiled. "It's been nice knowing you, Cath."

"You too, Bea. You too."

"All right. Now that you two squared all your affairs, let's take a look at the enemy." My aunt opened her big book to the first place she had marked with a napkin. *"Opacum Diabulus."*

"A-Am I reading this right?" I stuttered. "Does this say that this thing grants immortality in exchange for souls? How can you sell someone else's soul?"

"I'm glad you asked." Aunt Astrid grinned as she flipped to the next marked page. According to the history of the Opacum Diabulus, they preyed on people with narcissistic tendencies. "The Elderflower sisters seem to be rife with this affliction. When they played with the Ouija board, this thing and its minions were just waiting for the chance to slip through the portal. The problem is that these things were given an invitation. It's like inviting vermin into your house. Once they are there, it is impossible to get rid of them on your own."

"So we're like the exterminators." Bea put her hands on her hips and looked off proudly into the distance like a superhero.

"Yeah. That will be our nickname. Not Ghostbusters but the Exterminators. We sound like mafia henchmen."

"I'm glad you brought that up," Aunt Astrid said. "Like the gangsters in movies, you never get something for nothing. They require payment for their services. Unfortunately, Marie Elderflower was the first installment."

Bea and I just sort of stood there dumbstruck. The idea of trading in your own mother for the possibility of immortality was so foreign to us we couldn't quite wrap our brains around it.

"These things thrive on terror. Marie was essentially tormented to death. Her behavior could easily be called dementia, but she was not crazy. Those things preyed on her like the one that came from under your bed, Cath. Marie's severed toe and the insertion of the corn kernel and dead spider were part of the next payment plan. Like interest being added to the debt. The toe has to accompany the next victim. The corn and spider were to defile the body and prove loyalty," Aunt Astrid continued. "Or else the Opacum Diabulus will break your kneecaps or thumbs or whatever diabolical equivalent you'd like to use."

"So, if this group is really like a loan shark-y-slash-Al Capone-y organized crime outfit, are we risking retaliation?"

"Well, I think it is safe to say yes. You already had a taste of that, Cath." My aunt's face was grim. "But the Opacum Diabulus is only as strong as the people who summoned it. That is where we have a fighting chance of stopping this. The narcissistic personality type isn't a fighter. If we can get Fern and Gail away from their "protection," we can end this."

"How are we going to do that?" I asked.

My aunt flipped the book to the last page she marked with a napkin.

"We just need a diversion. We need to draw their attention then ambush them. It will require we split up." She pointed to the page in the book that held the only procedure known to extract the Opacum Diabulus or Gazzo, as I had grown fond of calling it. A movie reference made it easier for me to deal with. The slimy loan shark in *Rocky* was a spot-on image for me to visualize instead of the horrific black thing that crawled out from under my bed.

"There are only three of us. How can we split up?" Bea asked.

"Well, Cath has a bad ankle. She can't be left alone. So you will go with her. I'll handle my end."

"But Mom…"

"Bea, that little girl needs our help. She lost her mother in a very cruel and malicious way. Right now is a time for courage. Not selfishness. It's selfishness that brought this evil to us to begin with."

Bea nodded and took my hand.

"Besides, you don't think your mother has connections? I've got connections. You don't worry about me. Just make sure you do what I tell you."

Aunt Astrid read the remaining details from the book to Bea and me, and we made our plan. But as with all perfectly laid-out plans, there was a fly that desperately wanted to land in the ointment. In our case, it was the rain the following day.

## ❦ 21 ❧

### AMBUSH

We had all slept under Aunt Astrid's roof that night. Actually, it was more like a catnap, but she insisted we rest in preparation for the ritual we were going to have to perform the following morning. But as the sky started to lighten, I heard the first ping-ping-pings on the windowpane. It was raining. Normally, this would encourage me to pull the blankets up higher and roll over for a little more shut-eye. But not today. I sat bolt upright, flung off the covers, then jumped out of the bed only to land my feet on the floor with a cuss and growl. My ankle was still too tender to put much weight on. I grabbed the walker and behaved as if I were eighty years old.

"I don't believe this! Can you believe this? Rain?

Today, it has to rain! We couldn't get just one day of sunshine. Very funny, Universe! Very funny!"

*Hwwwaaa! Hwwwaaa! Hwwwaaa!*

I honked my horn in frustration.

Bea popped her head up from the sofa in the living room.

"Do you hear that?" I grouched. "Rain. So much for the sun minimizing the shadows."

"It'll be okay," Aunt Astrid said as she came out from her study, wiping her eyes awake and patting me on the shoulder. "They'll never expect us to do anything on a day like today."

I wasn't comforted by my aunt's words. I looked at Bea, who groggily scratched her head and waved good morning to me.

After a breakfast of Bea's special "before dangerous witchcraft" tea and toast with homemade lemon marmalade, we got dressed. Treacle, Marsh-mallow, Peanut Butter—whom Bea had brought over the night before after she brought Jake leftovers for dinner—Bea, and I then lined up and waited for my aunt to conjure up one of her strongest, most powerful protection spells.

So much sage was burned around us, I could barely see Bea standing next to me. The words Aunt Astrid recited were in a language I didn't know, but I could feel their power settling deep inside my chest and working their way outward.

I felt as if I could stand on a train track with an oncoming locomotive barreling down on me and stop it not with my bare hand but with just a look.

"Okay, girls. You've got your supplies, and you know what you are supposed to do with them. Get yourselves over to the Elderflower house and stay out of sight. This isn't a fight in which we want to use our hands. We want to engage the enemy as little as possible. It's an ambush. The element of surprise is our greatest ally."

"How will we know when you've got your end of the surprise set up?" I asked as I leaned over the top of my walker and grabbed a banana for the road.

"You'll know. It will be obvious. Just follow the instructions. Stay out of sight. I'll join you as soon as I am able."

It should be mentioned that my aunt Astrid didn't drive. She knew how, but it was rare to catch her behind the wheel because of her vision. The merging and melting of dimensions had the tendency to make her weave and dart dangerously in and out of traffic. She was the stereotypical "female driver" men warned their sons about.

Her part of the plan required she be at the Elderflower offices. It was early enough in the morning that they wouldn't be open, and foot traffic would be scarce. So no one would see her appear out of thin air. Teleportation was a very rare gift. Aunt Astrid explained it as opening a door no one could see and stepping through. The trick was knowing what door would get you to where you wanted to be.

"Now remember, we are supposed to stay out of sight. No matter what happens," Bea said as we parked the car down the block and tiptoed up to the Elderflower house. Our three familiars, who were sitting patiently in the back seat like little dolls, had come with us. But they quickly went to their posts and blended in to their surroundings so seamlessly I lost sight of them almost instantly. The overcast day gave everything a flat appearance.

"I got it." I hobbled with my walker. The thing made a click-click with every step. "I don't know how I am supposed to do that with this thing, but I certainly will blend in as best I can."

Bea pulled my hood up so it covered half my face. She did the same for herself before we ducked behind the neighbor's bushes.

"You stay here and hold the bag," Bea instructed as she pulled out a package of salt and seven black-onyx stones from the backpack she was wearing.

"After I put this stuff around the house, I'll end up just across the yard in the other set of bushes. I'll just wait there until Mom makes it clear she's done her part."

I felt as if I were on the sidelines and Bea was getting all the fun of playing on the field. Still, with the dampness of the air and the cold temperature, my ankle throbbed. It was a little better than yesterday, but it wasn't good enough for me to be much help. Not until the chant. I was needed for that. But up until then, I was just a weirdo limping along through the bushes.

So as Bea started off and began barricading the Gazzo and his henchmen in with salt around the perimeter of the property, I watched the house. I saw shadows moving inside. These were the real shadows of people moving around.

I didn't like the fact that Fern and Gail's luxury cars were parked in the driveway. They didn't live here and had houses in Sarkis Estates or some other sickeningly wealthy neighborhood. It really was hard to believe they were related to Evelyn, who was a sweet girl despite her rather ghoulish appearance.

Finally, I saw Bea turn up across the lawn in the other neighbor's yard. She pulled a tiny scrap of paper out of her pocket and waved it at me. I reached into my pocket, pulled out a similar piece of paper, and did the same. It was time to read the chant Aunt Astrid had provided:

*Catch this darkness.*

*Keep it in detention.*

*Within the salt.*

*Within the stone.*

We were to say this quietly and continually until Aunt Astrid arrived. Things were proceeding as planned, and I was sure that I saw a couple of the shadow people unable to resist the black-onyx stones being sucked into the thick, shiny blackness.

Then I heard the voices, and it changed everything.

"I want you out of my house!" It was Mr. Elderflower. His voice croaked as if he had been talking all night without a drink of water and was now trying to raise his voice. "This is my house! My house!"

"Shut up!" I heard a female reply. I couldn't tell immediately who it was, but I was sure it wasn't Evelyn. The voice was too mature. Too deep. "We're not going anywhere. You'll be the one leaving soon enough, old man."

It was obvious from the reply that it was either Fern or Gail. I tried to focus on the words, but I was having trouble.

"I know what you are!" Mr. Elderflower shouted. "You're evil! And I want you to leave my home and never come back!" It broke my heart to hear him saying those words. Fern and Gail were still his daughters. How hard this must have been. But what I heard next was even worse.

Something broke, like a heavy picture or maybe a small shelf. Something crashed to the ground. Gail and Fern laughed. There was no other way to describe that sound than diabolical.

"What are you doing to him?" It was Evelyn. I was sure of it. "Leave him alone! You're going to kill him!"

"You shut up!" Fern screamed. *Really* screamed. The only time I'd ever heard a scream as desperate as this one was when I saw a five-year-old having a tantrum at Walmart. That little girl had screamed at her mother with her eyes squeezed shut, her face red, and her mouth stretched as wide as it would go. Her little hands were clenched into fists, and her whole body was rigid with rage.

"This is all your fault! You're the one who is going to kill him! You worthless piece of garbage! We hate you! We hate you!"

"Stop her!"

"You're not leaving!" Another crash.

I looked around me, wondering if any of the neighbors heard this domestic disturbance. To me, it was as loud as a plane taking off, but nothing seemed to stir around the neighborhood.

I hadn't realized that I had stopped chanting. I looked at Bea, who was also hearing the commotion from inside. I could tell she was thinking the same thing as me. We couldn't just sit by and listen to this.

"Get off me! No! Leave him alone!" Evelyn screamed.

I stood up and walked out of my hiding spot. Surprisingly, Bea did the same thing. Clumsily, I hurried my walker toward her.

"Bea, we can't let Evelyn fight them alone."

"I was thinking the same thing."

We heard more laughter and the pathetic whimpers of Evelyn begging her sisters to leave their father alone.

"I'll do it! I'll do what you want! Just don't hurt him anymore! Don't hurt him!"

"What are they doing to that man?" Bea clutched my arm. I felt the strength of her character rush through the palm of her hand and into my arm.

"I don't know, but I've heard enough. Let's—"

Just as we were about to stomp like gangbusters into the Elderflower house we froze in our tracks.

From several oddly angled shards of darkness, half a dozen shadows came to life. They clawed and pulled themselves out of the darkness that they, themselves, were made of and began to approach us. The one with the top hat stood behind the rest. Its arms were dangling at its sides, and I was sure that was the same fiend that had come to my room. It just watched as its crew closed in on us.

"Any idea what we should do?" I looked at Bea, who had grown pale.

"No. But the element of surprise has been compromised."

"You think so?"

Bea scooped up the onyxes and quickly stuffed them in her jacket pocket. They were not going to free their evil brethren that easily.

"Call him an ambulance!" Evelyn cried from inside the house.

"Call him an ambulance. Call him an ambulance," the sisters said mockingly.

That was when Bea slipped her hand in mine and squeezed tightly. The look on her face was not of fear or regret but determination. I couldn't say the same for myself. I thought I looked rather foolish, but I squeezed her hand back.

"I couldn't live with myself," she whispered.

"Me neither."

We turned to step onto the Elderflower property to somehow beat our way through the shadow people to Mr. Elderflower's rescue. Hissing and horrible fighting filled my ears. Like the pitiful cries I'd heard in my ears the other night.

The shadow people stretched their arms and fingers, trying to reach us just beyond the circle of salt. Once we stepped over that line, we were in their territory.

The rules would no longer apply.

"To heck with this," I growled and tossed aside my walker. "I'm going down swinging. Evelyn needs us." I took one step over the salt, and my ankle shrieked in pain. But before I could change my mind and scramble back Marshmallow, Peanut Butter and Treacle darted from every direction into the Elderflower yard and dove into action.

"Come on!" Bea grabbed my hand and pulled me along the grass. I limped and ground my teeth, but finally, we made it across the grass and to the front door. She let go of my hand long enough to take hold of the doorknob and nearly tear the door from its hinges.

I wasn't sure if she had seen Opacum Diabulus or the Gazzo in the top hat ease backward, stepping into a shadow and disappearing. It couldn't be that easy, right? Treacle did scare him away before. Was this weird fear of cats all it took? Aunt Astrid didn't say anything about it or point anything out in her book. Why was it scared of the cats?

At this point, who was I to question a little good luck for our team? Our felines were holding the shadow people so we could get inside. To waste any more time would be ungrateful. So in we went. Tres-passing. Unlawful entry. Breaking and entering. I wasn't sure what law we'd just broken, but I was sure we'd broken at least one of these.

But when we saw what was happening inside the house, I didn't care what laws we broken. If there was ever a time for vigilante justice, this was it.

## ❦ 22 ❦

## POISONOUS VENOM

I had heard stories of people dying of a broken heart—a husband and wife had been together for over sixty years, one of them died, and it was only a matter of days before the remaining spouse did the same.

Seeing Mr. Elderflower's face, I knew I was looking at the face of a broken man. Whatever these girls had done to their father, I could not forgive.

"Cath." Evelyn sighed with relief as if she had been waiting for us or knew we'd eventually show up.

Bea stomped into the house with enough rage to set a high-rise ablaze.

"That is enough!" she shouted at Fern and Gail.

The grown women stood there in shock like two girls who had been caught with their hands in a cookie jar. For a second, I felt embarrassed for them. Here they were, two ladies in their early thirties with successful careers and material wealth, standing in front of my cousin with wide eyes and trembling lips as they tried to think up a lie to cover themselves.

"What have you done to him?" Bea demanded as she dropped her backpack to the floor.

"We didn't do anything," Fern scoffed, even though her voice trembled.

"It wasn't us. It was Evelyn. She can't be trusted to do something so simple as to help her father down the stairs," Gail added. "He probably fell again."

Bea was so enraged her body shook.

"Evelyn, did you do what we told you to do yesterday?" Bea asked loudly.

"Yes."

"Mr. Elderflower, can you hear me?" Bea never turned around to look at Evelyn or her father. She didn't take her eyes off Fern and Gail. "I need you to get to Evelyn's room. Right now."

"What did you do, Evelyn?" Gail demanded.

"Don't you raise your voice at her," I growled. My adrenaline was pumping so fast that I didn't feel my sore ankle anymore. Plus, I didn't want them to smell out that weakness. These were the kinds of sisters that would exploit my injury without hesitation.

Evelyn helped her father to his feet. He had a goose egg on his head, and his eyes looked nervous. He'd be okay. I was sure of it. Bea had him now.

As I watched Mr. Elderflower cling to Evelyn, I felt a terrible tug in my chest. All they had was each other. What kind of torture had these two spoiled brats caused?

"Dad, let's go." Evelyn helped him. He was an average-size man. That was a lot for a seventeen-year-old girl to lift all by herself. How sad it was to see this man whose pride was in pieces. He was embarrassed and humiliated. A person didn't have to be an empath to see that.

"Don't you take him anywhere," Gail ordered. "Leave him right where he is."

Bea stepped closer to the sisters. Had she had the chance to put her hands on them, I was afraid she would have crippled them with her anger. They recoiled from her.

"You will not harm them again," Bea hissed.

Both sisters started to laugh nervously.

"We haven't done anything to them!" Fern whined like a child. "They've done all this to themselves. And who are you people barging in our house? You better get out of here before I call the police!"

"Please," I replied calmly. "Call the police. Call and tell them the Greenstones broke into your house. There will be twenty squad cars out front in two minutes. You want that?"

"Yes," Gail snapped. Only after she spoke did she realize how pitiful she looked. She looked at her sister, who wasn't looking at her but was focusing on Evelyn and Mr. Elderflower as they started to go upstairs.

"Good!" Evelyn cried as she pulled her father's arm around her shoulder and helped move him upstairs. "Then I'll tell them what you've been doing."

"Sure!" Fern stepped in. "Like they'll believe you. You are a troubled teen, responsible for your mother's death. If you've got any marbles left in your head, they are rolling around, ready to fall out any second. They'll know you hurt Dad. Gail and I both saw it."

Evelyn's eyes were filled with tears. Without her Goth makeup and clothes, she looked helpless against these two bullies.

"I didn't kill Mom," she whimpered.

"Yes, you did. You and Dad wouldn't listen to us

and have her committed. Now she's dead," Fern said.

"Don't talk to her like that." Mr. Elderflower managed to speak, but his words were more like a suggestion and not a command from their father.

"I've heard enough from you two," I said and walked as if the pain in my ankle weren't there.

"Hurry, Evelyn," Bea urged. She sensed something, and it didn't take long for me to figure out what it was. "We have to hurry, Mr. Elderflower. Please. Hurry."

We had given Evelyn so much sage to burn in her room that it was the only safe place in the entire house. Bea took hold of Mr. Elderflower so Evelyn could get to the top of the stairs and hold her door open. I saw her legs buckle for just a second before regaining their strength. That was her energy leaving her body and going into Mr. Elderflower.

"Cath!" Bea yelled to me. "Hurry up!"

"You go on, Bea." I scowled. "I can handle things down here."

For a second, I was sure I could take these two women. They didn't look like as if cross-trained on the weekends or were especially toned or muscular. In fact, they looked rather doughy and soft around the edges.

"You have everything," I said. "You are both successful. You have money. Your own medical offices. What is wrong with you?"

"It's all fake!" Evelyn yelled. "Go ahead. Ask them where they got their diplomas. Ask them. They sold their souls for a bunch of fool's gold. I know it. They aren't smart enough to make it through junior college, but we're all supposed to believe they finished med school? Ha! It's all fake!"

Fern and Gail looked mortified. What had Evelyn meant, 'all fake'?

"Shut up, Morticia!" Fern screamed up the stairs. "Like anyone would believe you. I've got a calendar filled with names of people coming to see me. How is that fake?"

"Yeah!" was Gail's witty reply. These women became stranger and stranger every time they opened their mouths. If I hadn't been so incensed at what I heard them saying when I got here, I would be laughing at them.

I stepped up to face the Elderflower sisters and, for a moment, thought I was going to pull this off. My anger was so intense it was palpable, and they knew better than to take a step. But that wasn't it. That wasn't it at all.

From behind them rose a cloud of pitch-black

smoke. It twisted and turned like a thick bubbling liquid that finally formed into the Gazzo with the top hat. It towered between the two women, whose nervous faces suddenly transformed into sinister grimacing masks.

"So, is this your pet? Or should I say you guys are its pets." I swallowed, but there was no saliva in my mouth. The blackness was bottomless. Even the onyxes that hopefully held some of this demon's minions in it weren't as dark as this dark.

Pure blackness and devoid of even the slightest speck of light, the thing became a solid form.

Fern and Gail watched with glee as I stepped back cautiously, wincing as the pain in my ankle nearly tripped me up. It was no good that I had to steady myself against the staircase banister. It was obvious I was injured. To them and the Gazzo, I was like a bird with an injured wing. I was easy prey for a skulking feral cat or hungry raccoon.

It was bad enough to have a black, demonic entity slowly approaching, but it was worse when it flicked open its eyes.

As if I could ever forget the red slits that glared at me in my bedroom. I found myself staring into those same smoldering coals. Slowly, it peeled back a layer of darkness to reveal razor-sharp teeth. Its grimace had a shocking resemblance to the Elderflower sisters, who were watching with sadistic fascination as the thing came closer to me.

"You're not so tough now, are you?" Gail sneered. "Look at you. You're pathetic."

"Yeah, pathetic," Fern joined in. Maybe this wasn't the time to take notice of such a small detail, but I couldn't help but think these two women suffered an arrested development. Their comments and actions and replies were not the thoughtful words of grown-ups. How did they interact with their clients at work? Did they make snarky remarks at them too?

Obviously, I couldn't focus on that for too long when I had the paranormal equivalent of a kneecap breaker approaching me.

"She's going to go just like Mom," Fern said.

I held my breath.

"Yeah." Gail giggled. "Too bad we won't get to watch this one go a little crazier by the day. Running back and forth, turning lights on in all the rooms. Not sleeping for days at a time. That would be funny."

"It's going to squeeze your heart until it pops." Fern laughed. "Like a tick."

Their laughter echoed in my ears as the blackness

began to overwhelm me. My heart was racing. I felt the heaviness I had in my bed. My strength was running out of my body as though someone had turned on a faucet and just let the water run. Invisible weights had been attached to my legs, my shoulders, and my arms, and I was sinking to the ground. No matter how hard I tried to crawl up just one step, I couldn't do it. I was on my knees. My back was against the banister, and I tried to call for Bea, but nothing would come out. But my eyes remained open, and my brain was alert. It wasn't sleep falling over me. I was stuck in a spider's web and had been pierced with the poisonous venom that paralyzed my body but allowed me to see and understand what was happening. The sounds of many voices screaming and arguing came from its open, grinning mouth.

"Once it's done with you, it's going to get your partner in crime," Fern said, jerking her thumb upstairs. "I wonder if there is a way we can take over that coffee shop they own."

"We'll have to get the old lady that works there to sign it over to us," Gail suggested. "Then we'll keep her working there while our friends watch her twenty-four hours a day. She'll lose her mind after she signs over the deed. It will be easy."

"The real fun will be watching Evelyn go," Gail hissed.

"Yes. She'll be convicted of murdering our father and sent away for a long time. Our friends will follow her to the prison. She'll ramble and scream for them to leave the lights on. The other inmates will grow to hate her because she's crazy. Her good looks will be gone in no time. They'll find her hanging by her bed sheet or a pair of shoelaces or something."

They laughed. It made me sick to my stomach to hear it. But I was fading. There was nothing I could do except keep this thing occupied long enough for Bea to help Mr. Elderflower. Then maybe Evelyn could have them all shimmy down the tree outside her window to get away.

"Say goodbye." Fern waved at me.

"Yeah. Hasta la vista, baby," Gail added.

Just as I looked into the red eyes and saw myself reflected in them, I heard a familiar voice.

*"Get away from her!"*

It was Marshmallow. Behind her came Peanut Butter. They dashed up to me and stood on either side of my head. The Gazzo flinched backward but bared its teeth at both cats.

Then Treacle came in the front door. He was

puffed up to almost three times his normal size. His green eyes stared at the beast.

"*I know you,*" he growled loudly. His tail whipped back and forth. I felt as if I were in some parody of a Clint Eastwood spaghetti western and there were going to be a shootout between my cat and Gazzo.

Slowly, the weights were coming off my limbs.

Marshmallow and Peanut Butter snarled and swatted at the thing and at the sisters. With every inch the blackness receded from me, the more of my strength returned.

"Don't just stand there. Get a broom," Fern ordered. She stepped forward and tried to kick Marshmallow away from me but instead got a long, healthy gash along the side of her leg from the cat's sharp claws. "Ouch! I'm going to skin you alive for that." She put her hand over the blood coming from the wound.

"I don't think you'll do any such thing," I said as I started to push myself up.

Gail returned from the kitchen with a broom and began swiping at the cats. They darted back and forth, away from her clumsy swings.

That was when I noticed her feet. She was wearing Evelyn's combat boots. She was the one who'd broken into my house.

I gulped at the air. I could smell the sage burning upstairs. It was like a shot of vitamin C. The familiar pain in my ankle was there, but I was thankful for its sobering effect.

As Gail swung the broom, I grabbed ahold fast and yanked it clean out of her grip. She let out a yelp of surprise.

Meanwhile, Treacle and the Opacum Diabulus had engaged in a screaming match. I understood Treacle's threats.

*"I beat you back before! I'll do it again. And you'll never return! Never!"*

The horrible shouts and cries that poured out of the Gazzo's mouth sounded like the hopeless cries of lost souls, making me shiver. But I had to focus on the Elderflower sisters. Now I had a broom. Would it be enough? It had to be.

"Get the black one out of here!" Fern ordered her sister. "It's the black one! Get it out of here!"

"I'm trying!" Gail whined as she tried to kick at my cat. That was it. Finally, still wobbly on my feet, I took the broom and swiped it at Gail's feet, causing her to land with a thud on the hardwood floor.

Fern made a wild, clumsy dash at Treacle. She reached for him with her hands curled like claws. She grabbed my cat and pulled him to her by the scruff of his neck. Treacle hissed and growled, scratching madly but missing his attacker.

"Not very tough now, are you?" She puffed up with pride and turned to hand over my beautiful feline to the Opacum Diabulus. The Gazzo. I was terrified as I stepped up to the thing. Holding my breath, I stuffed the fear way down deep, spun the broom in my hand like a ninja, and channeling every bit of energy I had, swung for the fences. The hard end of the stick contacted Fern's face with a solid crack. A home run.

"Ouch! Oh oww!" she cried, dropping Treacle and reaching for her face.

Treacle fell to the floor, landing on his feet. With Marshmallow, Peanut Butter, and me, he cornered the top-hat-wearing specter. Before Fern could get her bearings, I grabbed Bea's bag that she had dropped at the door and pulled out the bag of salt.

Gail tried to scramble over and yank it from my hand, but she had hit her forehead so hard she stumbled over her feet. There wasn't much left in the bag. A handful at best. I hoped it would be enough as I threw it at the Gazzo.

As I expected, it was like buckshot tearing little pieces of blackness away, revealing an angry, fiery inside. It peeled its lips back in agony, and the hundreds of voices that bellowed all at once from inside its mouth shrieked in pain and infuriation.

It recoiled and writhed in a grotesque manner before it swiped long black talons at Fern and Gail. Then it rushed to a corner, where it stood glaring at all of us before blending into a normal shadow and disappearing.

"What have you done?" Gail wailed. I whirled around and saw her gaping at Fern.

"What have I done? You are the one who couldn't stop a cat!"

My head was beginning to pound. These two sisters didn't know any other way to communicate. It was shouting, or it was nothing.

"Where did it go? Call it back! Call it back, Fern!"

"It's not coming back." I started to giggle. Aunt Astrid must have succeeded at her end. I couldn't wait to hear the details. "Looks like your bodyguard isn't as tough as a couple of cats and three ladies." I burst out laughing and pointed at Fern and Gail as the cats came and stood protectively between the Elderflower sisters and me.

"It's not gone." Gail was near tears. "It's not gone, Fern. We need it. We've come so far. I'm not going back to the way things were!" she screamed, making my head throb.

"Shut up, Gail! I'm trying to think!" Fern shouted.

"Don't tell me to shut up! You shut up!"

"I've had enough of you, Gail! Just shut your mouth!"

It was as if they had forgotten I was even there. I would have liked to laugh at them. It would have been so easy to take this time to twist the knife a little. But I didn't. In fact, I grew more and more uncomfortable with each insult they traded.

Evelyn was right. Everything about the Elderflower sisters was a lie. They were not professional or successful or smart. They were a con. They were a complete hoax on everyone around them.

I didn't laugh at them. I felt a sad queasiness in my gut that made me want to run away and hope to never see them again. I opted to scramble upstairs. A train of cats followed me. I knocked quietly at Evelyn's door while Gail and Fern continued their argument downstairs. I wondered if it was going to come to blows.

## ❦ 23 ❦

## CROCODILE TEARS

Evelyn opened the door and smiled at me.

"Can you feel it?" she asked.

"Feel what?" I smirked as the cats slipped inside the room, past my feet.

"The air. It's like we can finally breathe again." Her eyes were red but dry.

"How are we doing up here?" I asked, wincing as the sisters continued throwing insults and threats at each other. Mr. Elderflower was sitting up. The color had come back to his cheeks, and he looked visibly younger than he had on the floor when we'd first arrived. He still had the goose egg on his head, but his eyes were clear.

"Well, Dad and I are good. I think your sister is wiped out."

"She's actually my cousin. But I think of her as a

sister." I stepped inside. The smell of sage was comforting. It had kept the Opacum Diabulus and his goons from entering Evelyn's room. But when I looked at Bea, my heart nearly stopped.

"Hey, girl," she said. Her face was ghostly pale. She was sitting on the floor, leaning against the bed.

"I think our work is done here, Bea. Let's get you back home."

"Okay. But I don't think I can walk down the stairs without stumbling," she admitted between chuckles.

"I'll help you, Bea."

"Mr. Elderflower, are you sure?"

"I'm positive." He stood up, and I gasped at the transformation. It was as if he'd grown an entire foot in height, and his shoulders were like those of a linebacker. He bent down and scooped Bea up as if she were just a child.

Evelyn got the door, and I slipped out ahead to make sure the coast was clear.

Gail towered over Fern, who was sitting in a green armchair, rocking back and forth. I wasn't sure if it was a trick of the light or what, but they seemed to have changed since just a few minutes ago. Their makeup was garish, and their clothes looked as if they didn't fit right, either too tight or too loose.

They stopped what they were doing and stared at their father. He set Bea down, and I quickly looped her arm around my neck to help her stay up. My ankle was killing me, but Bea needed my support. She was exhausted and suffering from severe burnout.

"Fern! Gail! Shut your mouths!" Mr. Elderflower shouted. He sounded like a drill sergeant. He sounded like a father that had been pushed to the limit. The two ladies froze.

"Evelyn, call the police."

Evelyn's eyes nearly popped out of their sockets.

"I'm sorry, girls." Mr. Elderflower stepped closer to his bickering daughters. "Your mother and I did our best. We were never rich people, but we loved you. Somehow, that wasn't enough. You're just bad."

"It was Fern's fault." Gail began to sob gallons of crocodile tears. "Oh, Daddy. She made me do it. She told me we'd be rich. She said—"

"Do you really think, after all that has happened, I'd believe anything that came out of your mouth?" Mr. Elderflower asked quietly. "Evelyn, give me the phone, honey."

I watched as Evelyn dialed 911 and handed the phone to her father. Nothing had changed in Fern or Gail. They glared at their baby sister with the same hatred of the snake for the woman in the garden. They weren't sorry.

"Hello. Yes. I need the police at my home. My daughters tried to kill me. I suspect they killed my wife, who passed a few days ago. Also, they have been practicing medicine without the proper licenses."

I squeezed Bea around the waist and nodded toward the door. Treacle walked ahead of us, pushed the screen door with his paw, and held it open with his body.

"Such a gentleman," I said.

"Meow!"

Bea insisted on picking up the onyx stones that we had used in our restriction spell. She inspected them and grinned. There were several shadow people trapped inside them. She could see their shapes shifting and thrashing just beneath the shiny surface.

"Aunt Astrid will want these," she said.

"You wait here. I'll go get the car."

"What about your ankle? Oh, Cath. You have got to be in some serious pain."

I looked around the yard and saw my walker lying on its side exactly where I had tossed it. I hopped over to it, bent down, set it upright and squeezed the horn.

*Hwwwaaa! Hwwwaaa!*

The sounds of sirens were quickly approaching, so I hurried to the car. The adrenaline kept me going. Just as the squad car pulled down the Elderflowers' street, Bea was slamming the car door shut, and we quietly and slowly pulled away.

No one needed us anymore. What would we say? That we'd had this threefold plan to rid the Elderflowers of the menacing Opacum Diabulus that sort of went sideways for a while but all was well that ended well? Yeah, our cats were the real heroes of the day. Scout's honor.

"I hope Mom is okay." Bea rubbed her forehead.

"We'll know soon enough." I looked at the back seat. The cats were snuggled together with their eyes narrow slits, and their motors could be heard purring with the car engine.

"So, what happened up there?" I asked.

"You wouldn't believe what that man had inside him. To be honest, I don't know how he was still alive. There were parts of his aura that were nearly black. If they were a physical part of his body, I'd call it gangrene." She blinked as her eyes welled up. "Those girls had been torturing the family for years. But it all came to a head when Evelyn started planning for college. Remember, she said she was a straight-A student. That was a slight understatement. By the time she turned sixteen, she had invitations to three universities, one of them Dartmouth."

"That little morbid chick?"

"Yeah," Bea chuckled.

"All broody and black, and here she is with a genius IQ. Isn't that something?"

"Yeah, to normal people, that is impressive. But Gail and Fern were beside themselves. They had already been dabbling in things they shouldn't have been."

"But how did they get the things they had? The offices? The cars? They wore designer clothes, and their hair and makeup were always done." I scratched my head. "When Evelyn yelled that it was all fake, she was right. Mrs. Elderflower was the first one to question their acquisitions. She thought they were hookers."

A burst of laughter rocketed out of my throat before I could catch it.

"I'm sorry. They just don't strike me as the hookin' kind."

"No. They don't. But they don't strike me as a dermatologist or a veterinarian either. But that's what they were telling everyone. They forged their diplomas and transcripts. But the Opacum Diabulus gave them everything else. The offices. The big houses and cars. Even their youthful appearance. It was all a mirage."

"No one suspected anything weird?"

"Yes. Marie did. According to Evelyn, she walked in on Fern and Gail practicing some kind of black-arts ritual in the basement of their house. That was when the shadow people started showing up."

"They summoned them, like Evelyn said."

Bea nodded and fidgeted in her seat. She wanted to get home to make sure Aunt Astrid was okay. I pushed the accelerator farther down.

Bea continued telling me the Opacum Diabulus helped make everything look beautiful and shiny and new. They made patients submit their will while they were in their offices and not realize they were being robbed of their money and parts of their soul. It was the action of truly selfish hearts.

"Marie tried to help them, but it was too late. They were too corrupted."

"Wow. I can't imagine it. I can't imagine wanting something so badly I'd be willing to kill for it. It's a concept I can't wrap my brain around."

As we drove the rest of the way home, I told Bea about my skillful maneuvers with the broom. We laughed at that. But when I described how Fern and

Gail turned on each other, we finished the rest of the drive to my aunt's house in silence.

We were delighted to see her front door was open. All the cats trotted in before us. But while Bea staggered as a result of her burnout and I hobbled with my walker, the pain in my ankle reaching the level of excruciating, the quiet that came from inside the house suddenly gripped our hearts.

## 24

### BLACK MASS

"Mom?" Bea stepped inside first. "Mom!"

There as no answer.

"Aunt Astrid?" I propped the walker next to the door. It was easier to hop using the furniture to balance than try to struggle along with that contraption.

Bea ran upstairs to check those rooms.

I searched the spare room and the downstairs bathroom before I got to the study. I found her lying on the floor, facedown.

"Bea!" I screamed. Her footfalls could be heard pounding across the ceiling. Quickly, I fell to my knees and rolled her over. Putting my head to her chest, I listened.

"I can't hear anything." I started to cry. "Bea! I can't hear anything!"

Bea's face was pale already. But when she saw her mother lying on the floor, I was afraid she was going to faint.

"I can't hear her heart, Bea." My hands trembled as I reached up for my cousin. She rushed to her mother's side. Rubbing her hands fast back and forth, she began her second examination of the day. How much more could she take?

I watched her hands and her eyes. It was as if she were folding dough in the air or conducting an orchestra only she could see.

"Mom!" she yelled. "Mommy! I've got it!" Bea's right hand clenched into a tight fist. "I've got it, Mommy! You can breathe! Breathe!"

As though she were starting a lawnmower, Bea pulled and yanked and tore at something I couldn't see. I couldn't help at all.

"Let go!" Bea yelled. "She isn't yours!"

With one final wrench, Bea fell backward, and my aunt gasped for air. Her coughing and choking and gulping big breaths were like music to our ears.

"Mommy!"

"Oh, Bea. Cath. You girls." She pulled us to her and held us tightly. "For a minute there, I wasn't sure I'd see you again."

We all caught our breath and let the tears and adrenaline subside before any of us spoke.

"Aunt Astrid? What happened?"

"Well, let me tell you—it was no Fourth of July picnic." She smiled and looked at my ankle. "Cath, that thing has swollen terribly. My gosh. What were you doing? Playing soccer with them?"

I chuckled and shook my head.

"Bea, honey, you need to lie down. Immediately."

"I'm okay now, Mom."

"No, you are not. Come on."

Aunt Astrid instructed me to put my pajamas on and go lie in her bed with a pillow under my foot. She took Bea into her bathroom and ran her a bath. None of us spoke of what happened until Bea was in her pajamas too and we were both in my aunt's giant, cozy bed.

"I'll put on some tea," she said soothingly, brushing our hair away from our foreheads.

"Aunt Astrid, aren't you going to tell us what happened?"

"Of course. But let's have a little tea first."

I looked at Bea, who blinked her heavy eyelids at me. Somewhere between that and my aunt walking out of the room, we both fell dead asleep. When we woke up, Peanut Butter and Treacle were on either side of us. The sun was either just setting or just rising. I couldn't tell.

Bea still looked pale.

I looked at my foot. The swelling had gone down a little, so I decided to get up and seek out my aunt. I found her sitting in the kitchen with a steaming cup of tea in front of her. The *click, click* the walker made with each step caused her to look up.

"How are you feeling?" she asked.

"Better. I guess I needed that rest."

"Of course you did." She got up and pulled a teacup from the shelf. Before I could sit down, she had the cup steaming and steeping in front of me.

"You gave us a fright, Aunt Astrid." I choked back tears. "What happened?"

She took her seat next to me and let out a big sigh.

"Everything had gone as planned. I reached Fern's office and began the ritual to peel away the façade that coated the entire place while Uncle Eagle Eye did the same at the vet office. We could see each other through the haze of the dimensions. Not clearly. Not perfectly. But I could recognize his build and that head of white hair anywhere." She sipped her tea. "It felt like he was really there. I almost forgot that I had summoned him, not unlike the Elderflower girls did with the Opacum Diabulus. Except Uncle Eagle Eye was my husband. I talked to him on Worm Moon. At least I thought I did."

Fear seized my heart.

"Just as the walls started to decay and fall, as I suspected they would once the ritual was in motion, I saw it. The black mass with the top hat."

"Aunt Astrid, Bea and I went inside the Elderflower house. I know you said we shouldn't, but if you heard what we did, you wouldn't have stood by. It was horrible."

My aunt looked at me with her lips pinched together.

"It's too late to change things now," she replied, looking into her teacup. "The dismantling of the Elderflowers' smokescreen was successful. The buildings look like bomb shelters now. The patients that went to either office will probably file class action lawsuits for fraud. I don't see Fern or Gail getting around this. If they don't kill each other, they will probably spend the next several years in jail."

"But what happened to you? How did the Gazzo find you?"

My aunt told me that the shadow creatures had the ability to move freely from the Elderflower home to the offices and back again thanks to Fern and Gail, who confused their success with having control over these demons.

"As I watched the doctor's office crumbling apart, I looked across the dimensions to see Uncle Eagle Eye. I felt like a young woman again. In my heart, I longed for it. Just a few minutes to hold his hand or even just hear his real voice. It's amazing how easily the heart can be tempted." She cleared her throat.

"Since you and Bea had engaged the creature, it tried to stop me. But not with the same terrifying face it showed you. Instead, I saw the face of an angel. For just a second, I wished your uncle were with me again. That was all it took. A second. And that thing with the top hat pounced. It grabbed hold of my heart as the last weeds grew up through the floors, as the last tiles fell from the walls and crashed into a million pieces."

She told me she flew through the dimension to the vet office and found it in the same deteriorating state but Uncle Eagle Eye wasn't there. She wrestled with the beast, but it wasn't going to let go. It was in a rage that its hosts had been not only discovered, but bested.

"I felt its grip around my heart," she said.

"That's what the Elderflower girls said it did to their mother. It squeezed the life out of her heart." I swallowed. "We brought that to you. I'm so sorry, Aunt Astrid. I'll never do that again. I'll never disobey you again. I promise!" I cried. "We thought we were doing the right thing. Really, we did."

"I know you did, Cath." She smiled sadly. "You and Bea have been the joy in my life so long I can't remember anything before you. If you broke the rules, I'm sure you had what you thought was a good reason. But sometimes the best of intentions have dire consequences that you could never foresee, even if you had the gift of foresight." She winked at me.

I felt so exhausted I couldn't even smile back at her. There wasn't anything I could say that would make this any better. So I didn't say anything more. I just listened.

"So I ran through the dimensions with this demon clawing and grappling with me. I knew if I could just get home, I might have a fighting chance. It screamed at me the entire time." She shook her head and looked at her teacup.

I knew what she was talking about. I heard those same horrible voices.

"The last thing I remember was stepping through

the door. I don't remember walking through the house or getting into the study. The next thing I knew, I could breathe, and my girls were home with me."

"Bea did it," I said. "Bea was sick after dealing with Mr. Elderflower. It took everything she had to help that guy. You should have seen him after she helped him. Part of his aura had gangrene." I was babbling. "But he looked ten years younger and was even able to carry Bea down the stairs before he called the cops on his daughters."

Aunt Astrid looked at me strangely.

"She could barely walk. All she wanted was to make sure you were okay and get home. Then when we found the door open and you didn't answer, she freaked out. She ran upstairs, looking for you. We finally found you, and she didn't hesitate. She jumped right in and saw the Opacum Diabulus. At least, I assume she did. She didn't tell me. She just kept yelling at it to let you go. That you weren't its property. I swear, Aunt Astrid, I don't know where she found the strength."

My aunt leaned back and looked at me.

"It was my fault we went into the Elderflowers' house. She wouldn't have done it if I hadn't pushed."

I swallowed so I wouldn't start crying. I knew Bea and I had both agreed to go into the house. But what did I do? I swung a broom around and made smart remarks, and if it weren't for the cats, the Elderflowers would probably have had my head mounted on their wall. Bea was the hero of the day. She should be treated like one.

My aunt looked at me then at her teacup and then at me again. "Maybe you should go back to bed, honey. It has been a long day."

"Yeah, okay." I wiped my eyes and grabbed hold of my walker.

"Would you like a piece of chocolate pie to help you sleep?"

I shook my head no.

"Cath, we all make mistakes. The Elderflower girls made mistakes, but they were never corrected by their parents. Look at how they turned out."

"Do you think I could ever be like those girls?"

"No. Because you have people around you who love you enough to tell you when you are wrong."

I nodded and went back to bed. As I snuggled up to Treacle, I held in my tears. I didn't want to wake Bea. She'd ask all kinds of questions.

"*You were amazing today. That move with the broom*

*was fantastic."* Treacle purred and rubbed his head against mine.

*"Thanks."*

I couldn't help it. I was glad someone noticed. Even if it was just my cat.

# EPILOGUE

By Valentine's Day, all of us had more or less recovered. The café's tacky pink-and-red décor instantly cheered me up as I went in to open with Bea. She was already behind the counter, putting out Kevin's delicious muffins, cookies, and brownies.

"What are your plans for today?" Bea wriggled her eyebrows at me.

"Nothing much." I shooed her as I wrote the lunch specials on the chalkboard. "We're not cheesy like you and Jake. What are you going to do, feed each other chocolate-dipped strawberries and spout off bad love poems you wrote for each other?"

"Ha ha. That was last year."

I laughed.

After we unlocked the doors, our regular started

trickling in. They were delighted by Kevin's intricate Valentine's Day cookies in the shape of anatomically correct hearts. They were on sale only today, and from the look of the sales, we'd be out by lunchtime.

Tom came in dressed in his uniform.

"I'm here to see my best girl before work." He leaned over the counter to give me a kiss on the cheek.

I blushed because he had done it with a small lineup behind him. A group of pre-teen girls giggled. Love was indeed in the air.

I gave him his coffee and a bag full of Kevin's finest to go. "See you later then."

"Pick you up on the dot." He leaned in again to whisper in my ear. "I can't wait, because massages are involved tonight."

My blush deepened. Bea had taken over the cash register, smirking to herself as she gave the next customer change. I ignored her.

After the morning rush died down, a familiar face appeared. Well, sort of. When she came in, I didn't recognize her at first because she didn't have her goth makeup on. Fresh-faced, she was dressed in a plain white T-shirt and jeans, but she still had on the black Chucks.

"Evelyn!" I exclaimed. "How are you?"

Evelyn beamed as she approached us. "Great. Dad is doing better now. He's even going to the gym." She lowered her voice. "I never thought life could be good again. I'm glad the shadow people are gone."

"You're telling me," I said. "They were horrifying. You're brave for living with them all these years."

"I don't know if bravery had anything to do with it," she said.

"You're dressed differently," Bea remarked.

"Yeah." Evelyn nodded. "It was the shadow people's influence, and I didn't even realize it. I don't feel the need to wear so much black anymore. I feel a thousand pounds lighter."

"You're certainly glowing like an angel," I agreed. "Here, try one of these cookies, on the house."

"And what do you want to drink?" Bea asked.

"One of your healing drinks, please," Evelyn said. "Whatever you make, I'll drink."

Bea smiled. "Coming up."

After I gave Evelyn the heart cookie, she took it out of the bag and examined it, giggling. "Realistic rendering. I didn't know your baker was such an *artiste.*"

"He's full of surprises, that guy," I said.

Bea handed her a to-go cup. "Lavender tea with

an extra dose of something. You can tell me what that something is the next time you come in." She winked.

"Come in anytime," I said. "We're related, remember? Somehow, anyway."

Bea looked thoughtful. "That's right. We really should figure out how."

Evelyn looked sad for a moment. "Well, I lost two sisters, but I gained two new ones." She lowered her voice. "Who are *not* trying to kill me."

I didn't know whether it was appropriate to laugh, but Evelyn broke into a huge smile.

"I better get to school." Evelyn waved. "Thanks for everything. See ya!"

"Bye, sweetheart."

Bea and I watched her walk out the door, and then we went back to work.

## ABOUT THE AUTHOR

Harper Lin is the *USA TODAY* bestselling author of 6 cozy mystery series including *The Patisserie Mysteries* and *The Cape Bay Cafe Mysteries*.

When she's not reading or writing mysteries, she loves going to yoga classes, hiking, and hanging out with her family and friends.

www.HarperLin.com